8/17

Rog

Book Four
Tru Exceptions Series

WRITTEN BY
Amanda Tru

Walker Hammond

Publishers

Rogue, Tru Exceptions, Book 4
Copyright © 2016 by Amanda Tru

Published by Walker Hammond Publishers
ISBN-13: 978-0692618097
ISBN-10: 0692618090

Also available in eboook publication

PRINTED IN THE UNITED STATES OF AMERICA

Chapter 1

Kelsey knocked firmly on the door.

This was not going to be pleasant. She would rather be locked in a windowless office with a mountain of paperwork than knocking on Garrett Matthews' door.

She waited, wondering if she should have put the confrontation off until morning instead of coming here directly after she arrived in D.C. But, no, even with the light dwindling to night, she wanted to get this over with.

Kelsey heard a lock turn, and the door opened to reveal the tall, dark-haired, ridiculously handsome man she was unfortunate enough to be seeking. And to make matters worse, he was dressed in a tux.

Kelsey raised her eyebrows. "I take it I'm interrupting your plans.

"What do you want, Johnson?" Garrett growled impatiently.

Though his face remained impassive, Kelsey saw the corner of his lip curl up slightly in annoyance, which gave her a thrill of perverse pleasure. Even though she hadn't wanted this assignment, the fact that her mere presence had the power to annoy and aggravate this man was a definite plus.

Kelsey raised her eyebrows. "I take it you're going out."

"Yes." Garrett's eyes raked over her harshly, from the toes of her boots, over her black leather jacket, to the top of her dark head that didn't even reach his shoulder. "And you clearly aren't dressed for the occasion."

Kelsey hadn't expected a friendly greeting. There had never been anything close to affection in her relationship with Garrett. But, animosity, on the other hand? They didn't even require words to have that in spades.

"Andrews sent me," Kelsey said, not bothering to sugarcoat her presence. The faster this went, the quicker she would be rid of him and the sarcasm, attitude, and ego that went with him. Just pull the band aid off quickly and get it over with.

Granted, Garrett probably already knew why she was here.

He cocked an eyebrow in question. "And?"

"Your orders are to report back to New York." Kelsey stated matter-of factly, working to keep her features as expressionless as his. "You have a new assignment."

Garrett's stoic expression didn't change, but his breath released in a scoff of derision. "You wasted a trip. I already got the memo."

Without another word, he started to shut the door in her face.

Kelsey stuck her boot in the door frame, stopping it from closing shut. "I don't think you understand, Agent Matthews. I wasn't sent to deliver a message. My orders are to deliver *you* to New York."

"Oh really?" Garrett said, his passive face suddenly transforming with the dawn of an amused grin. "Why didn't you say that in the first place? My plans can wait a bit. By all means, come in. Come in."

He opened the door wide and grandly bowed in welcome as she entered.

Feigning confidence with a haughty look Garrett's direction, Kelsey entered the house. It was actually more of an old bungalow that sat behind a large plantation-style house. Garrett rented what Kelsey guessed had once been a guest house to the main one.

Though the house itself may have dated back to the 1800s, the bungalow was quite modern inside. With a single glance, Kelsey swept her surroundings, mentally cataloguing every detail she saw, even while turning back to face Garrett.

The interior was not at all what she expected. She had somehow thought to find a typical bachelor's pad with clothes piled everywhere and takeout paraphernalia littering all surfaces. But instead, her quick assessment had revealed a room that was so neat and clean, it was almost stark.

However, instead of impressing her, his tidy housekeeping increased her dislike for him. Kelsey wanted to dislike Garrett, and wanted to have evidence to justify that emotion. So, in this case, she resented the fact that his cleaning habits hadn't given her a good reason to dislike him all the more.

Garrett shut the door behind Kelsey, turned and casually leaned back against the door frame with his arms folded across his formally-clad chest in a thoroughly relaxed posture. "Please tell, Agent Johnson. How exactly do you intend to fulfill your assignment?"

"Obviously, just asking nicely isn't going to do the trick," Kelsey said, idly walking into his living room. "So that leaves me with a few other options."

Simply desiring to get under his skin, she began thoroughly inspecting every item in the room. She lifted each frame on the wall, looking behind it before letting it fall back to a slightly crooked position.

As she meandered, she spoke. "I somehow get the feeling that all of my charm is lost on you; so simple persuasion is out."

She paused, putting a finger to her lip as if seriously pondering her options. "Seduction?" she mused, looking directly at Garrett before turning back with a feigned shudder. "I just don't have the stomach for it."

Reaching the couch, Kelsey casually sat and turned to a stack of sports magazines neatly arranged on an end table. With each one, she lifted it up, glanced at it, and tossed it haphazardly beside her on the couch.

"Drugging you?" she continued idly, as if carefully considering each tactic. "Nope, forgot to pack my supplies."

"So that leaves using my brilliant logic to convince you to come, threatening you, and sheer force." As she spoke, she stood, ticking each option off on a finger. "You're a stubborn jerk of a guy, so I'm sure you'll just refuse to come on principle, no matter what I say to convince you. And threatening you I'm sure will get the same reaction. So that leaves… "

"Forcing me," Garrett finished with eyebrows raised." He slowly, deliberately walked over to where she stood, stopping mere inches from her and looking down from his height, clearly challenging. "And how exactly is little miss, Kelsey Johnson, going to do that when she can't even manage to qualify to be a field agent?"

Anger flared, and she barely kept a lid on her reaction. It was true that she wasn't a field agent, but for all he knew, she wanted it that way. The truth was, she had no idea why Andrews had sent her to fetch Garrett. The director of their Homeland Security office was one of two other people on the planet who knew exactly why she wasn't a field agent. And in Kelsey's mind, that should eliminate her from ever having an assignment like this.

None of this should have been surprising to Andrews. Undoubtedly, their boss also knew that Garrett's refusal to comply with his orders was inevitable. Added to all of that, Kelsey and Garrett's mutual dislike was not a secret to anyone.

So, just how had he expected Kelsey to bring Garrett in?

When Kelsey had initially asked for clarification on her assignment, Andrews had simply instructed, "Bring him in. Whatever it takes, preferably not in a body bag." He had paused, as if wanting to say more, but then he shook his head and pursed his lips, like he didn't want to say too much. He looked her directly in the eye and said, "I need him alive. You'll figure it out."

And now here she was, standing toe-to-toe with Garrett, with no idea what she should do. She talked big, but it was all an act. Garrett was one of Homeland Security's top agents for a reason. Realistically, Kelsey was a desk clerk who worked back-up for field agents who did the real work.

What would Rachel do? Kelsey suddenly wondered. Kelsey didn't have many friends, but the one person she considered her best friend was also the best field agent Kelsey had ever seen. At Kelsey's insistence, Rachel had taught her to shoot and fight better than any Homeland Security trainer could have.

It didn't take much thought for Kelsey to realize exactly what Rachel would do. After all, Kelsey had witnessed Rachel in a similar situation where she'd felt it necessary to prove herself to

Garrett. If Rachel was here now, she'd take Garrett down suddenly and quickly, letting him continue his conversation from flat on his back.

Just as the idea popped into her head, she saw Garrett startle, his eyes flying open wide. Kelsey's immediate thought was that he had somehow read her intentions.

Then she saw a little red beam of light dart along the edge of her vision.

Garrett threw himself at her, knocking her to the floor as the room was riddled with bullets.

Chapter 2

The sudden impact knocked her breath out. Garrett stayed on top of her, covering her body with his as she gasped for breath. She couldn't see anything past the wall of Garrett's body, but she could hear the terrorizing staccato of gunfire.

After the initial barrage of fire, Garrett finally rolled off her and, in one smooth motion, curled into a crouched position with a gun in hand. Staying low, he scurried to position himself between the door and the now-shattered front window. Following his lead, Kelsey drew her weapon and scrambled to the other side of the window.

Kelsey watched Garrett for a sign. Taking a baseball cap off of a rack near the door, he looked at it soberly.

"If you can help it, Johnson, don't shoot to kill."

"What are you talking about, Matthews?" Kelsey hissed.

In every single training in which Kelsey had ever participated, that one rule had been drilled over and over. As a Homeland Security agent, if you fire your weapon, you always shoot to kill. The risk is too great otherwise.

"Didn't they just shoot at us?" she whispered fiercely. "I kind of got the feeling they weren't just shooting for—"

Garrett tossed the baseball cap into the air in front of the window. It was instantly hit with multiple bullets as it tumbled to the floor.

Before the echoes of the shots had died down, Kelsey and Garrett simultaneously pivoted toward the window, peeked out far enough to get a line of sight, and started firing. Kelsey immediately realized that Garrett really hadn't needed to be concerned about them killing someone. It was dark enough outside that she couldn't see a thing through the shattered window. So she fired a bunch of bravado shots—all show and no effect—until the fire was returned.

Watching, Kelsey waited the briefest of seconds before ducking back. At the answering shots, her gaze had caught on pinpricks of light.

"To the right!" she yelled to Garrett."

She couldn't pull the trigger before something sailed through the front windows and rolled to a stop against a wall.

Immediately, it began hissing as it leeched a gray cloud into the room. Garrett scrambled across the floor. He quickly pulled up a plank in the hardwood flooring, revealing a large, hidden cavity. He reached in and then tossed Kelsey a gas mask.

Even as she put it on, she knew they didn't have much time. The gas meant that their enemies would be breaching the house soon, expecting to find them passed out. Though the masks would keep them conscious, the house was surely surrounded and they had no way to escape

She looked back to Garrett, finding him still on the floor, pulling out weapons from what was apparently his own personal arsenal. He slid two other guns across the floor to her, but she had no idea why. What use were they if he didn't want her to shoot to kill?

He gestured for her to follow him.

She grabbed at him, catching the end of his suit jacket before he hurried away. The lights had gone off with the initial attack. With smoke filling the room, Kelsey was afraid if she let go a physical connection, she would lose track of the man in a gas mask and black tux.

She shuffled along behind him like the caboose on a train. She heard the screech of a door opening, and then he bent down to the floor. He lifted something up and climbed down into what looked like a trap door. Kelsey waited until his entire shape was swallowed up in blackness, then a little light flickered on at the bottom of the hole.

"Hurry!" he called, motioning her to follow him down.

Kelsey found the ladder and quickly climbed down the rungs. When she reached the cool air of the bottom, Garrett went partially back up the ladder to pull the trap door shut.

Without a word, he turned and began walking swiftly down a tunnel.

Kelsey didn't know where they were. With Garrett's little light as the only illumination, she couldn't see anything beyond the narrow ray that flickered in front of Garrett as he walked. Everything beyond that little dancing beam was pitch black and indiscernible.

The air smelled earthy and musty, like it had been stagnant for a long time. There was also dust in the air, probably from their disruption in the seldom-used tunnel.

Garrett kept a good pace, though Kelsey's heart rate was still out-distancing it. How long would it take their attackers to figure out they had escaped through a trap door?

Figuring they were now safe from the gas, Kelsey pulled off her mask off so she could speak. "Where are we?" she asked, calling ahead to Garrett.

Garrett pulled his mask off as well. "This is an old escape route for the underground railroad. There is a larger room by the entrance to the tunnel that was used as a hideout where the slaves could stay. The house itself has been modernized; I'm not sure if it was even a house when the tunnel was originally in use. But with whatever changes they've made to the exterior, they've kept the trap door to the tunnel. My landlady is an old friend of my mom's. She told me about the tunnel with its entrance in the hall closet, but swore me to secrecy. Though much of the original land belonging to the plantation was sold off, the tunnel sets entirely within the five acres that still remain. This escape route is one of the major reasons I wanted the house."

"Just in case bad guys decided to shoot up the place and you needed to escape when they filled it with gas?" Kelsey asked sarcastically.

"In our line of work, you can never be too paranoid," Garrett replied quietly.

Garrett's vague reply annoyed Kelsey. She needed to know who was after Garrett, but he apparently wasn't willing to volunteer any information without an inquisition.

Just as Kelsey was about to launch into the task, Garrett stopped walking. Through the flickering beam, Kelsey saw another ladder leading up. Garrett climbed up the rungs and pushed to dislodge the door above. It finally gave way, but not before dumping its load of dirt and dust on both Garrett and Kelsey's heads.

Moonlight spilled into the tunnel as the door came open. Garrett hurriedly hefted himself up into the night air, and then reached down to help pull Kelsey up. He then tossed his gas mask down the shaft. Kelsey followed suit, tossing hers down the hole as well. Garrett promptly shut the opening and rearranged the plants disguising it on top.

Kelsey looked back in the direction of where the house should be. Through the thick overhanging trees and bushes surrounding the tunnel's exit, she caught sight of the bright orange glow of flames.

Kelsey gasped, "Matthews, they're burning your house!"

The glow of fire was far enough away that it didn't provide any light to read Garrett's expression.

"I guess that renter's insurance wasn't a waste after all," he said calmly. He turned away and started walking. "They couldn't find us, so they obviously are making sure no person or evidence survives."

"Evidence?" Kelsey asked, immediately latching onto the word. "What evidence? Who exactly is after you, Matthews? And why in the world would someone burn down your house?"

Garrett ignored her, simply increasing the speed of his footsteps.

Kelsey ran after him. "Why aren't you answering? I can't help if I don't know what's going on!"

"I don't need your help!" Garrett gritted out. "But since I now appear to be stuck with you, I guess I'm the one who's going to need to help you not get killed!"

He stopped and hurriedly began rummaging in the underbrush, as if trying to uncover a large object hidden there. "Look, those men who set fire to my house are going to be very thorough about searching this entire property. I will tell you everything as soon as I get us out of here, preferably with no bullet wounds."

Kelsey breathed deeply, trying to hold down instant fury. Maybe it wasn't too late to use Rachel's tactic and put the man flat on his back. However, as much as she would like to, she knew he had a point about getting out of here. Though she didn't know what he was doing, she helped brush aside leaves and branches from what was hidden in the brush. An inquisition and any bodily harm to Garrett would have to wait for later.

Garrett pulled the object out, the flickering of his flashlight catching on wheels, a handlebar, and shiny metal.

"You get the dorky one," Garrett whispered, shoving a helmet Kelsey's direction.

They were going to make their escape on a motorcycle.

Garrett got on and nodded his head toward the rear, indicating Kelsey should get on behind him.

Kelsey strapped on the helmet, which did resemble a rather dorky bowling ball, and obediently climbed on.

"Hang on," he instructed.

Kelsey stiffly positioned her arms on either side of Garrett's waist, hating the tingle that shot through her, even through the layers of his suit.

Before she had talked her arms into doing more than just sitting there, the headlights flipped on, and Garrett gunned it. She grabbed him tightly to keep from falling off, immediately and uncomfortably aware of the firm muscles beneath her hands.

The bike ripped through the dirt of an overgrown lane. Without slowing down, Garrett cornered as the lane met the concrete of the main road. Kelsey held tight for the curve, but couldn't relax her hold at all as Garrett's speed steadily increased.

Though she didn't think they had been followed, she didn't dare look behind them. Their enemies probably weren't aware of the old access road at the back of the property and were probably still busy with the fire instead.

It was strange that Garrett still thought they would search for him. That meant that the purpose behind setting fire to his house hadn't been to kill him. Garrett had mentioned evidence. What kind of evidence could Garrett have that would require extermination by arson?

Even though they seemed to have no pursuers, Garrett took no chances and rode a complicated route of turns through side streets and residential areas. His speed had slowed, but Kelsey still had to maintain a firm hold, never sure when and where he would make a sharp turn.

They finally turned onto what Kelsey thought she recognized as the Baltimore-Washington

Parkway, and she felt relieved for two reasons. First, with help from all of the maps in her head, she was reasonably certain she knew exactly where they were. Second, they were going north out of the DC area, and north meant New York.

Trees lined both sides of the roadway, creating ominous black silhouettes beyond the streetlights. Even though Kelsey hadn't caught sight of anyone following, she couldn't relax. She still needed to deliver Garrett to New York, and with what appeared to be a well-armed militia intent on killing him, that task was looking more impossible than she had initially estimated.

With city lights fast approaching, Garrett exited the roadway and turned in to a gas station. He parked along the side that bordered trees and was empty of other businesses.

He quickly dismounted, and Kelsey followed suit, removing her helmet and looking around. Though they were parked in the shadows, light from the streetlights caught the shiny chrome of the motorcycle. Kelsey glanced over the vehicle, recognizing the make and model. This was a top-end piece of machinery and carried a corresponding weighty price tag, which was interesting since she had never seen Garrett with a motorcycle before.

"BMW K1600 GTL," Kelsey said, identifying the bike. She let her voice carry a hint of curiosity, almost as if she was posing a question.

Kelsey watched in the dim light as Garrett's eyebrows raised.

"Why am I surprised that you know about motorcycles?" he smirked. "Agent Johnson is good with facts. She collects facts behind her desk all day long. Lots and lots of facts."

"Are the insults your attempt to distract me from what is very likely stolen property?" Kelsey challenged, raising her eyebrows to match his.

"I borrowed it from my parents," Garrett admitted finally, frowning. "Of course, Dad didn't know I needed it for a potential escape vehicle."

Kelsey knew that Garrett's parents were retired. Garrett was right in that she was good at keeping details in her head, and she remembered Garrett taking a few days off a couple years ago to attend his dad's retirement party. A sudden image of an older couple in matching outfits riding a motorcycle came into her head, and the corners of her mouth lifted. Garrett's motorcycle-riding parents might be the kind of people Kelsey would like to meet, though the fact that she would need to go through Garrett to do so was a definite drawback.

"So if you were planning for an escape, that means you knew someone was coming after you," Kelsey said casually, hoping to get him to talk.

"I didn't know for sure, but yeah, when Andrews called and pulled me off the case, I knew things might be going south, fast."

"Who—"

Garrett held up a hand to silence her as he began digging through one of the storage compartments on the motorcycle. "Please don't pester me yet with questions, Johnson. Obviously, this still isn't the place to talk."

Garrett pulled things out of the pack and hurriedly threw them on the ground, looking for something specific.

Sure enough, Kelsey spotted a couple of matching, lime green, lightweight, motorcycle jackets join the collection on the ground.

Kelsey was tired of playing Garrett's games. He obviously had a plan, but didn't feel the need to fill her in on it, or even let her know who was chasing them. Besides that, he was being rude. It wouldn't hurt him to tell her what was going on as he looked for whatever he needed.

Feeling completely done with Garrett and this assignment in general, Kelsey took out her phone and dialed.

"We need an extraction," she said simply.

Garrett whirled around and grabbed her phone. He threw it to the ground, crushed it with the heel of his foot, then picked it back up and threw it as hard as he could into the trees.

"What are you doing!" Kelsey shrieked, grabbing at his arm as he tossed the phone.

"What are *you* doing?" Garrett spat back.

"I was calling New York! The fastest way to get out of danger is to have a team come and extract us. Then we can figure out what's going on."

"Wrong!" Garrett hissed. "The fastest way to get *in* danger is to have a team come and extract us!"

"What are you talking about! We need to get to New York! Andrews will know what to do."

"We are not going to New York."

"Maybe *you* aren't going to New York. But I am. I'm done. If Andrews wants you to come in, he can send a different agent who doesn't mind being shot at and berated. You can go ahead and stay out here and get yourself killed, for all I care. I'm not following you on some misguided mission being chased by bad guys trying to kill you. And I am definitely not going rogue and disregarding Andrews' orders. I'm leaving!"

Kelsey stepped toward the gas station. Someone in there was bound to have a phone she could borrow.

Garrett's hand closed on her arm, whirling her back to face him. "No, you're not." Instead of angry, Garrett's voice was now low and deadly serious. "You don't seem to understand, Johnson. You don't really have a choice. We're stuck together. You already made your choice."

"What are you talking about?" Kelsey asked, completely exasperated. Through the feeble light, Kelsey caught a hard glint in Garrett's eyes and an almost mocking curl of his lip. The look sent a chill slicing through her.

"You made your choice back at my house when you took your weapon and shot back. You see, those weren't technically enemy agents. Those were American special ops. Kelsey Johnson, the second you fired on your own men, you committed treason. So yes, Agent Johnson, I am going rogue. But you are going with me."

Chapter 3

Kelsey stared at Garrett, opening and closing her mouth, but no words came out. She had fired on her own men?

And now she knew why he'd said not to shoot to kill!

Garrett placed his hands on her shoulders and looked her in the eyes, as if willing strength into her to either not kill him or not fall apart. At the moment, not killing him was more of a struggle.

She wasn't going to fall apart. Kelsey Johnson didn't fall apart. Ever.

But she was angry. And as soon as those annoying sparks of electricity shooting from Garrett's hands against her shoulders stopped, she would gather up her wits and make sure he understood the full extent of her anger.

"Wait here," Garrett said, his eyes still reflecting his uncertainty about releasing her. "We don't have much time, and I need to go get something. I promise, as soon as we're safe, I'll explain everything. I'll be right back."

He reluctantly let go of her shoulders and turned toward the line of trees. But after taking a few steps, he turned back around and spoke softly. "Kelsey, I'm not the bad guy. Please trust me."

His whispered words floated across the distance, even as he disappeared amongst the dark trees.

Kelsey drew in a deep breath and released it slowly. She didn't want to be here. She didn't want to go on the run with Garrett. She hadn't intentionally fired on her fellow Americans. They had been shooting at her first! She was sure if she explained the situation, she wouldn't be held at fault. Besides, wouldn't they be in the wrong as well? They had opened fire on two Homeland Security agents. She was sure Andrews would be able to sort everything out.

Yet, she would be showing back up in New York having not completed the assignment Andrews had given her. Should she really leave Garrett and return to New York? Her mind reviewed Andrew's orders. She recalled the look on his face as he'd paused, then said, "I need him alive. You'll figure it out." It was almost as if he'd wanted to say more.

Had he known that Garrett's life was in danger? Had he specifically sent Kelsey to help protect him?

And with that thought, Kelsey knew what she had to do. She would stay with Garrett, no matter what. Though she couldn't be sure, her assignment now made sense. Protecting someone was something Kelsey could do. Andrews knew that. If someone important needed protection, Andrews sent Kelsey. That was the only time she did field work. Andrews also knew that Kelsey would fulfill her assignment. In her entire career, she had never returned to Andrews from an assignment empty-handed. Andrews always seemed to know more than he let on. The fact that he had sent her to Garrett told her that he intended for her to stay with the other agent and protect him at all costs. Then, when it was safe, she was to deliver him back to Andrews in New York.

And that was the assignment she would fulfill, likely in spite of the man himself.

Kelsey automatically began picking up the items Garrett had strewn across the ground and putting them back in the storage compartment. Maybe it didn't matter, but she didn't imagine Garrett's parents would appreciate having their things thrown in the dirt.

Suddenly, the hair rose on the back of Kelsey's neck. She didn't see or hear anything, but it was a feeling of unease. Since this wasn't the first time she'd felt this warning, she knew better than to ignore it. She slowly turned, her training taking over as she inventoried every detail of her surroundings.

A car without lights on melded into the shadows of the building. Another, smaller shadow moved on the other side of the gas station.

"Matthews!" Kelsey yelled, not even bothering with trying to be subtle. If their pursuers were here, then it was already too late.

She jammed the helmet onto her head and mounted the motorcycle. She could hear Garrett crashing though the trees. He would know the only reason she would blow their cover was if there was imminent danger.

She started the motorcycle, rolling as close to the tree line as possible. She estimated they had about five seconds before they were surrounded.

Garrett bounded out of the trees and leapt onto the bike.

Kelsey took off. Shadows ran directly for them. Lights of vehicles flashed on, blinding in their intensity. Kelsey veered around the shadows of men on foot and hit the road without pausing her acceleration. Shots rang out, and she swerved.

Unfortunately, they didn't make it back on the road without company.

Kelsey raced through the city streets, taking corners that made Garrett's driving from earlier look tame. Seeing an alley, she turned sharply, knowing it would be too narrow for a car. They exited the darkness back onto a street, only to find a car blocking their way.

Kelsey screeched around it, barely missing it, and taking to the wide sidewalk for a block before turning down another street.

"Where's your watch?" a sudden voice in her helmet demanded.

Of course! Garrett's parents had their helmets equipped with speakers so they could talk back and forth. Garrett likely hadn't made the feature known before because he hadn't wanted to talk and face Kelsey's inquisition.

"They're tracking us somehow."

Unfortunately, what Garrett said made sense. Their government issued equipment could be tracked, but only by Homeland Security. But Kelsey didn't waste time analyzing potential implications.

Keeping her right hand on the handlebars, Kelsey reached her left hand back to Garrett. "Take it off," she instructed, holding her wrist still as Garrett fumbled to release the watch.

The weight of it fell off her wrist, and then Kelsey felt the balance on the bike shift with the motion of Garrett hurling it far away.

"Do you have anything else issued by Homeland Security?" the voice in Kelsey's helmet questioned. "Or anything else that could be tracked?"

"The only other government-issued possession I have is my gun, and I'm going to keep hold of that."

A dark sedan swerved into Kelsey's lane ahead of her. It stopped horizontal, completely blocking the road. Kelsey slammed on the brakes, and the tires skid as the bike fishtailed. She knew they were being pursued from behind, and now everything ahead was blocked. That left only one option.

Before the bike came to a stop, Kelsey hit the gas, pulling out of the skid and gunning toward her only escape. Unfortunately, the only road that didn't appear blocked off was the entrance back onto the Baltimore-Washington Parkway.

She flew onto the thoroughfare and saw that it was clear, but she felt no relief. She hadn't wanted to get on this road. At this time of night, traffic was sparse. Though there was no one to hinder their speed, that also meant that they would be fully visible on a straightaway with very few exits and nowhere to hide.

"You're not going to outrun them," the voice in Kelsey's helmet said.

"They'll have a blockade before we can make it five miles," Garrett continued.

"Then I'll take the next exit and try to lose them in the side streets," Kelsey said.

Though she easily maneuvered through the other cars traveling the road, she realized that lack of a close pursuit didn't mean safety. Besides, she had spotted at least one car and another motorcycle keeping tail a ways back.

"Chances are good that they'll have every exit going north blocked off before we get there," Garrett said, disagreeing with her plan.

"Blockades on main thoroughfares and every exit? Just who are we dealing with, Garrett?" Kelsey said frustrated.

"Someone who is capable of all that and much more," Garrett answered gravely. "They know you're with me. I'm sure that's how they found us. They traced your government-issued phone and watch.

If what Garrett was saying was true, there was no way for them to escape.

Kelsey had the motorcycle wide open, pushing it to the limits of its speed capabilities. Kelsey knew the specs on the machine—it was a fast motorcycle. And yet, according to Garrett, it wouldn't be fast enough. She wasn't worried about other vehicles outrunning or even keeping up, but they wouldn't need to. They were still as trapped as fish in an aquarium.

The instant the idea popped in her head, Kelsey slammed on the brakes.

"What are you doing?" Garrett yelped.

Kelsey watched her rear view mirror, carefully controlling the bike as the tires squealed and a car passed with horn blaring. Waiting a half second for the vehicles tailing them to be in the right position, Kelsey swung the motorcycle around 180 degrees, facing oncoming traffic head on.

"New plan, Matthews. Hang on."

Kelsey hit the gas hard, gunning the engine and keeping the force of her entire weight firmly on the gas pedal as the bike accelerated past the screeching motorcycle and sedan.

She focused on the lights of the oncoming vehicles, barely noticing Garrett's frantic prayers filling her helmet. The bike had great maneuverability, and the tricky thing about going the wrong way on a major roadway was not so much swerving around oncoming vehicles as it was doing it at over 100 miles per hour.

Kelsey's heart pounded, but her hands were steady.

If they could just make it to the next exit, they just might have a chance.

Two sets of headlights approached, side by side on the two lane road. There was no time to make it to the road's shoulder.

Kelsey's ears filled with the sound of Garrett literally screaming in terror. Instead of breaking or swerving, she leaned low over the bike, pushed the gas harder, and aimed in between them.

By mere inches, the two cars passed on either side of Kelsey's legs. The air from the passing cars was a physical force, like a vacuum that wanted to suck them off balance. Keeping her balance and control of the bike, Kelsey finally slowed enough to make the sharp turn onto an exit.

As they were deposited onto a city street, Kelsey was relieved to see that the way was clear. She had purposely gone past the exit they had previously taken for the gas station, figuring that knowing they were heading north, their pursuers would have taken measures to stop them that direction, but exits south should be open, as long as they made it there before their enemies had the chance to regroup from Kelsey's change of direction.

"Where are we going?" Kelsey asked, needing to know a destination. Garrett had obviously had a plan before they were ambushed at the gas station.

"Baltimore," Garrett said, rattling off an address in a raspy voice.

Kelsey's mind immediately sorted through maps, plotting a course that would keep them off main thoroughfares, yet would also not involve little-used roads that would draw attention to their travels.

"Pull over," Garrett suddenly demanded.

"We don't have time," Kelsey argued. "The longer we stay in this area, the greater chance they will figure out which exit we took. I can get us to Baltimore."

"Pull over!" Garrett repeated, his tone fierce.

Kelsey obediently pulled to the side of the road, seriously angry at the man. Did he not think anyone else capable of driving a motorcycle? He had to do it himself?

But instead of insisting that she move out of the driver's seat, Garrett hopped off the bike, rummaged around in the pack he had slung around his back, and then quickly replaced the old license plate with a new one.

As he shoved the old plate into his pack, the streetlights revealed his shaking hands. He bent over as if he was ill and his stomach might revolt. Then he took two deep breaths and hopped back on the bike behind Kelsey.

Kelsey may not have taken out his legs and put the man flat on his back, but at that moment, seeing him so shaken from the motorcycle ride felt even better.

Garrett didn't speak another word the rest of the drive to Baltimore. Kelsey was content to remain silent too, at least for the moment. After realizing that her job was to stay with Garrett, she also knew she would unfortunately have an excess of time with the man. She would make him thoroughly answer her questions sooner or later, and for now, she was content with later.

Instead, Kelsey focused on remaining alert for any potential danger, and getting them to the address in Baltimore. The only thing that made her current task difficult was a very acute awareness of the man behind her. When they were being chased, Kelsey hadn't noticed his arms around her, but now, the firm pressure of his hands around her waist made her both want to squirm and allow herself to lean back into the shelter of his strong torso. A tingling sensation extended from Garrett's touch, filtering through her body and out her extremities. It was almost like a laugh that couldn't be contained, or maybe an itch that couldn't be scratched. Either way, Kelsey didn't like it. It required extreme concentration on her part to keep on-task and not pull over just to get some distance from Garrett and the awful tingles from his proximity.

With great relief, Kelsey realized they had reached the right address. She pulled to the side of the street and stopped, turning to look at the large warehouse-type facility.

She removed her helmet to get a broader view. "What is this place?" she asked.

"A shipping distribution center," Garrett replied, also removing his helmet.

"And we are here because…?"

"We're hitching a ride on that truck over there," Garrett said, pointing to a large semi parked in front.

"And how are we going to do that?" Kelsey asked skeptically.

"I know a guy," Garrett said easily. "He left the trailer in this position away from the others and unlocked. In a few hours, this truck will be loaded and driven exactly where we need to go."

Deciding to hold her further questions, Kelsey followed Garrett to where he pulled up the back of the trailer and climbed in. Moving to the back of the cavern, Kelsey saw several large refrigerator-sized boxes.

"This is perfect," Garrett said with satisfaction. "The motorcycle will just fit in this box."

Kelsey again followed Garrett as he headed back to get the motorcycle. Before they arrived, his footsteps slowed and he spoke thoughtfully.

"Kelsey, where did you learn to ride a motorcycle like that?" he asked.

Kelsey took perverse delight in hearing the strain that marked his voice. She knew he wasn't referring to their more recent ride, but to the chase. He had been completely terrified, and that somehow pleased her.

With a steady tone, Kelsey replied matter-of-factly, "I like facts. I sit behind my desk and collect facts." And with an ever-so-slight taunting edge creeping into her voice, she finished slowly. "Lots and lots of facts."

Garrett tipped his head back and laughed, leaving Kelsey to be thankful that this wasn't a residential part of town. If anyone had been in the area, Garrett's laughter couldn't have gone unnoticed.

Garrett let the matter drop as they worked together to get the bike in the bed of the trailer and into the box at the back.

Kelsey found herself watching his face as they worked. Not that she could see much. The bright moon had snuck behind a thick layer of clouds, and they didn't dare use a flashlight. But when Garrett had laughed, it had almost seemed as if Kelsey could see sparkles of light coming from his eyes. Kelsey had never seen Garrett laugh much, and she found herself wanting to watch those sparks of light dance.

Of course, after realizing the direction her thoughts had taken, Kelsey immediately got angry at herself and once again began mentally rehearsing all of the annoying attributes that comprised Garrett Matthews.

Seemingly oblivious to Kelsey's thoughts, Garrett securely taped up his bike in the large box, and then turned and began positioning the slightly smaller box next to it

"What goes in there?" Kelsey asked. Instead of spending so much time messing with the box, shouldn't they be looking for a place to hide?

"We do." Garrett answered, bowing formally and gesturing that she was welcome to enter the large box.

"No," Kelsey said flatly, shaking her head and backing away. Riding with Garrett on the motorcycle had been more than uncomfortable. There was no way she was going to shut herself in a box with him for hours!

"Come on, Johnson," Garrett said impatiently. "I don't recall claustrophobia being in your file. This is the only way. Tom will make sure these two boxes are delivered to the right destination and then left alone."

"Couldn't you come up with a better travel plan?" Kelsey grumbled.

"My original plan didn't include two people," Garrett admitted. "It just so happened that I still had my mom's motorcycle gear, but I hadn't exactly planned on company." He looked at the box and shrugged. "It might be a bit of a tight fit, but we aren't exactly traveling."

"Then what are we doing... exactly."

Even though Kelsey couldn't' read his features in the scant light in the trailer, she could feel his amusement even before he said a word. "We're mailing ourselves."

Chapter 4

"I want my own box," Kelsey demanded.

"Sure," Garrett replied easily. "Go get yourself one."

Unfortunately, there were only two boxes in the trailer, and as much as she'd like to, Kelsey had to admit that breaking and entering a shipping distribution center to find herself a box probably wasn't the wisest course of action.

"Tom followed my request and provided two large empty boxes," Garrett explained. "If you ship yourself in a third, there is no guarantee you won't be rerouted along the way."

Sighing, he lost his lighthearted tone. "Come on, Johnson. I already had the plan in place in case something like this happened. I went behind the gas station to retrieve a stash of supplies I had hidden there—burner phones, license plates, IDs, and such. I used one of the burner phones to call Tom, but I didn't have time to submit a revised version of the plan to include two people."

At Kelsey's silence, the impatience in Garrett's tone was fast converting to anger. "I don't understand what your problem is. Being uncomfortable on missions is part of the job description for being an agent. And sitting in a box for a few hours doesn't rank in my top fifty of bad situations."

Kelsey folded her arms across her chest and glared at him, though most of her seething look was likely lost in the darkness. "But, remember, as you so like to remind me, I'm not a field agent. I'm used to my nice, cushy office chair behind a desk."

Garrett chucked. "I promise I won't bite."

"No, but I might," Kelsey grumbled, finally relenting and sliding past him to climb into the box.

Kelsey hunkered down in the corner while she heard Garrett slide the door to the trailer closed. He then came, took off his suit jacket, and climbed into the box with her. Kelsey watched as he, using his flashlight to see, poked a bunch of holes in the cardboard of the side facing the back of the trailer.

She shuddered at the thought of being completely shut in the box and needing those air holes. Garrett had been right in that she wasn't claustrophobic by nature, but she didn't think there was a scientific name for the condition she was suffering from—fear of Garrett Matthews.

Done with the holes, Garrett prepped the box opening with some tape, but stopped short of actually shutting it. "I think it is fine to leave this open for a few hours," he said. "But just in case we get some unexpected visitors, I'll need to shut it in a hurry."

Kelsey really wanted to suggest that they also not bother getting into the box for another couple of hours, but she knew it would be useless. There was always the possibility of that unexpected visitor, and they needed to take every precaution, which meant the right side of her leg in complete contact with Garrett's. At least he sat across from her, which meant that she could very easily kick him with her boot if the need arrived.

Garrett leaned back, loosened his tie, and unbuttoned the first few buttons of his dress shirt. Finally, he switched off the flashlight, and sighed. "Alright, Johnson, ask away. I have nowhere to go to avoid your inquisition."

With the absence of Garrett's little light, everything was devoured in black. Combined with the warm closeness of the box, it was almost oppressive. Kelsey wasn't even sure she could manage an interrogation of the deep masculine voice, especially if she couldn't study the man it belonged to.

"How about you just tell me what's going on," Kelsey answered. Talking would be much preferable to uncomfortable silence, but her energy was fading fast. She really didn't want to drag every last detail out of him if she didn't have to.

"Fine. But I have to assume that you already know more than you're letting on. Andrews always keeps you up to date on agents' assignments, and he sent you to get me. You must know what I've been working on."

"Andrews didn't debrief me on your assignment," Kelsey said, realizing that Garrett had assumed too much. "The last I knew, you were working on a case involving a potential political angle on the ring of American terrorists that Rachel and Dawson uncovered, but that was quite a while ago. Last I heard, the case was cold and you had no leads.

"It's the same case," Garrett confirmed. "After a solid year of dead ends, I finally struck gold about a month ago. Andrews would have never kept me on this assignment for so long if we hadn't been certain that something was there, even if we couldn't find it. Finally, I found an informant. Three days ago, he was supposed to hand over the evidence that would finally close the case. Unfortunately, he died in an apparent car accident before he was able to turn over the evidence."

Kelsey couldn't see his face in the dark, but she could hear the frustration in his tone.

Though his words had started matter-of-factly, as if giving a report, he was now unable to hide the bitter edge to his voice as he continued. "I am left with absolutely nothing. Thirteen months of work here in D.C., nineteen months since the attempted bombing in New York, and I have no evidence to incriminate an evil mastermind who is still free to plan atrocities."

"If you have no evidence, why does someone want to kill you? You indicated the strike team at your house was seeking to destroy evidence."

"They don't know that I have no evidence," Garrett explained. "I saw my informant's body. Some of his injuries were not consistent with a car accident."

"You think he was tortured first," Kelsey surmised.

"He was not an agent. He was a decent guy who was trying to do the right thing. They would not have had to push hard for him to tell them everything, including my name."

"But if he told them everything, they should know he didn't give you evidence," Kelsey objected.

Garrett hesitated. "The day before he was killed, I convinced him to finally give me names. I have nothing to substantiate what he told me, but I know who we're dealing with. And I'm sure that information alone is enough to want me dead. Of course, they also can't know for sure that I wasn't given evidence. There's no way they would take his word on it."

"Who is it?" Kelsey asked. She needed to know who they were up against. "You said the strike team sent to your house was from one of our own agencies. That means someone very high up must be calling the shots, literally."

Garrett was silent, as if reluctant to tell her.

"Matthews, as you said, they already know I'm with you. That alone seals my fate to be the same as yours. Even if we were to separate, they would come after me just as hard as they will you, because they will assume you told me everything. Our only chance is for you to actually tell me everything so we can figure a way out of this."

"You don't need me to tell you, Johnson," Garrett sighed, his tone resigned to the inevitable. "You should be able to figure it out on your own. It is rather obvious, isn't it? You probably just don't want to admit that the situation could be that bad."

"What do you mean?" Kelsey asked, feeling pinpricks of dread spread across her skin despite the stuffy warmth of the box.

"Think about it. We already knew we were dealing with domestic terrorists. That means someone would have to be in a position to gain something of value from that original bombing attempt in New York. Since that event over a year and a half ago, we've had a presidential election. At the time of the attempted attack, the presidential hopefuls were just earnestly starting their campaigns, gearing up for the primaries. Doesn't it stand to reason that a terrorist attack in New York might provide someone with publicity and ample opportunity to play the hero in the eyes of the American people?"

Kelsey thought carefully, following Garrett's logic. Slowly, she spoke, "The only presidential candidate from New York was the governor at the time."

"Yes," Garrett said, matching his hushed tone to hers. Had the bombing been successful, the national spotlight would have focused on New York, giving the governor the chance to appear compassionate, heroic, and decisive, which would then gain the trust of the American people and, most likely, the presidency."

"But that didn't happen," Kelsey filled in. "There was no bombing, and instead, not winning enough primaries, the governor became a running mate. And he is currently the vice president of the United States!"

"Exactly," Garrett affirmed, annoyingly calm.

"Matthews, do you hear what you're saying? You think Vice President Victoria Lewis is a terrorist?"

"I don't think it. I *know* it," there was not a sliver of doubt in Garrett's tone. "I suspected her for a while; like I said, it makes complete sense. But of course, I had no proof. Then it was confirmed by my informant, who handled finances in Lewis's inner circle. While not a part of the terrorist ring, he had come across emails and documents ordering the bombing in New York, and also a later one in D.C. When he went to extract the evidence, he must have tripped security, which got him killed."

Shivers raced up and down Kelsey's arms. If what Garrett believed was true, it was bad, very bad. "So I can see why she may have targeted New York," Kelsey mused, "but why D.C.? I remember a potential attack on D.C. was supposedly stopped seven months ago when Rachel and Dawson took out Rachel's brother, Phillip, and the rest of the terrorist ring, but why would it make sense for Victoria Lewis to order it?"

"We know very few details about that plot," Garrett sighed, his voice strained with frustration. "We don't even know for sure when it was to take place. She could have been targeting her running mate, intending to take his place. Whatever her plan was, I'm sure it was strategic. Whether a bombing at a D.C. location would yield an economic or political advantage, the only thing I know is that it would have benefitted Lewis."

"For Pete's sake, Matthews! I voted for the woman!"

Garrett grunted. "She's very good at what she does. She is poised, intelligent, and strong, but she is also diabolical. I do know that she and John Riley went to college together, but that doesn't count as evidence. She's the one we're looking for, Johnson. She's the head of a domestic terrorist ring, and probably guilty of many other illegal activities as well. Now, I just have to prove it."

"That's easier said than done!" The enormity of the situation crushed Kelsey with the sheer impossibility. "You're going after the woman who is one heartbeat away from being president of the United States! She already sent a U.S. team to take out their own agents. Every officer or agent we know—every good guy—is technically her employee. And she could probably just call in a drone strike, and no one will be the wiser. You and I both know what the capabilities are, and we also know there's a whole lot she can get away with, and no questions will be asked."

"You're not telling me anything I'm not already aware of, Johnson," Garrett said wearily. "It's my case. I've inspected it from every angle. I knew the risks, and when my informant was killed, I knew those risks were about to get very real. I got the message from Andrews, a formal order, to stand down and return to New York. I knew it wasn't an order he would willingly give. He knew I was close, which means the order came from above his head. I made my decision then, but it wasn't really a decision. I knew they would come to kill me. The only way out is to prove Victoria Lewis a traitor."

"There has to be something." Desperation tinged Kelsey's voice, and she didn't bother to hide it. "What is your plan? How are we going to get evidence against the vice president with the American government on our tail?"

"For the past three days, I've been scrambling to locate some new evidence. That's what I was doing when you arrived tonight. I was dressed up to attend a political fundraiser. Some of my informant's personal friends were supposed to be there. I hoped to observe them and find out if any of them had access to similar evidence and would be willing to risk their life to be a hero."

"But what is your plan now that Lewis is after you? How will you get the evidence?"

"I have a safe house ready. We'll make it there, and then we'll figure it out."

"That's not a plan," Kelsey objected, her frustration mounting. "How can you work for over a year and have nothing! No lead, no scrap? Matthews, I thought you were a better agent than that!"

Garrett let out an exasperated breath. "Look, Johsnon, my current plan consists of staying alive for the next twenty-four hours. I'm sorry if I'm a disappointment to you, but it's been a bad week. I know you've never liked me, even from day one. But I'm tired, you're tired, and in a few hours, we have the big job of not getting killed. Can you just curb your animosity and give it a rest for a little while?"

"Fine," Kelsey flung back, wishing she could turn and walk away. She really didn't intend to be so harsh with Garrett. Somehow all of her frustration and fear seemed to zero in with anger toward him. If she was being honest, she would have to admit that she admired him. He was risking his life to do the right thing. Up against a Goliath, he had stood tall, refusing to back down. Technically, he had disobeyed orders and committed treason, but to do otherwise would have been cowardly and a greater betrayal of himself and his country.

Without a doubt, Kelsey knew that Garrett would keep fighting this impossible Goliath, keep trying to find evidence to do what was right, until he breathed his last.

Deep down, Kelsey knew Garrett was a man to be admired.

Yet a grouchy, "Fine," was all she could manage.

She tried to turn away from him, leaning her body into the side of the box. She closed her eyes and hoped she could sleep to pass the time. But it was impossible to get comfortable. Every minute or so, she would readjust, seeking enough comfort so that sleep could come and steal her away from her thoughts.

"Alright, can you please stop wiggling!" Garrett groaned from where he'd at utterly still for the past five minutes. "Trying to sleep in a box is hard enough without having you flop around like a fish on caffeine! What is your problem?"

"Your feet stink!" Kelsey accused.

"My feet stink?" Garrett repeated, dumfounded at her response.

"Yes! But apparently that isn't your only problem! If you can't smell the toxins emanating from your feet, there is also something wrong with your nose!"

Kelsey suspected Garrett had slipped his shoes off to be more comfortable, but with his feet practically in her lap, the smell was nauseating.

"They aren't that bad," Garrett protested.

"If you don't have the decency to put your shoes back on for my sake, then do it for the sake of our safety. The second anyone sticks his head in this trailer, he'll know someone's here, just by the stench!"

"I am not putting my shoes back on!" Garrett said stubbornly. "Those are my dress shoes and are also known as torture chambers. They aren't exactly the footwear I would have chosen if I'd known I'd be going on the lamb. I'll put them back on in a few hours. In the meantime, I'll just switch sides so you can be upwind of my feet."

Before she could protest, Garrett had maneuvered around so that he was shoulder-to-shoulder with her, with feet pointing the same direction as hers.

Knowing that being rid of Garrett's entire presence was not really an option, Kelsey bit her tongue and tried to curl her body away from him into the other side of the box. But it was no use. She could still feel the heat from his shoulder on hers.

The foot odor was actually much better, but in desperation, Kelsey set her mind to focus on the smelly odor, trying to dispel some of the unreasonable attraction she felt dragging her toward the man she desperately wanted to avoid.

She closed her eyes and tried to block him out. He was silent, and she could only assume he was trying to sleep. She wondered if he even felt this tension that seemed to tie rubber bands of electricity between them.

Gradually, the silent darkness seeped into her tumultuous thoughts, and the beginnings of sleep crept around the edges of her mind. She still was thinking of Garrett, but her thoughts were much slower.

He'd said that she hadn't liked him from day one.

That wasn't true. She had liked him that first day, and that had been the problem.

Chapter 5

In between sleep and awake, Kelsey's mind drifted back to the first day she met Garrett Matthews. She was in college. After being approached about applying for a job with a government agency, Kelsey had consented to a series of tests that were supposed to match her with what job she would be good at.

Kelsey wasn't too optimistic. After all, some random guy in a suit had approached her at a job fair and handed her a card. However, she was desperate and needed to get money to continue school as well as pay for food, so she'd called and consented to the tests.

Spending a Saturday taking tests did not sound like fun, but she'd shown up at the office building, along with about ten other applicants around her age. They were all sitting in a waiting room when Garrett Matthews came through the door. With a smile that made Kelsey's jaw drop, he greeted them, identifying himself as the test proctor. He led them to a room lined with tables, where everyone found a seat.

Kelsey vividly remembered the instant Garrett first looked at her. He was holding the door for everyone to enter the testing room, and Kelsey was the last person in line. She looked up, and their gazes collided.

Kelsey caught her breath. In one second-long glance, the air sizzled with an attraction like she had never felt. Looking in his eyes, she felt as if she could see to his soul and somehow recognized him.

Then, like a light switch, Garrett's intense, gray eyes lost their spark, becoming monotone to match the rest of his demeanor. Whereas before, the man had been alive with vitality and personality, a mask slipped into place, concealing any hint of who he actually was.

Kelsey was left with the distinct impression that she had just been pushed out of a place she wasn't supposed to be.

Garrett shut the door behind Kelsey, and she found a seat.

Three hours later, Garrett announced the final exam. Thus far, Kelsey had taken tests on everything from math and science, to computer skills assessments, to a written essay test. For this last exam, the instructions were to answer the multiple choice test on the computer, print the screen showing their test completion, and then drop the paper through the mail slot; at which time, they were free to leave.

Kelsey thought the instructions were rather strange, but nothing about this experience had been normal. The test questions were rather deceptive. They appeared to be very simple, but Kelsey quickly realized several of them were meant to be trick questions!

"Psst!" the girl next to her whispered.

Kelsey lifted an eyebrow in question. There was supposed to be no talking during the test, but with Garrett Matthews out of the room, this blonde girl in a mini skirt was apparently willing to risk it.

"Help a girl out with number three!" she urged.

"The answer is 'E.'" Kelsey responded quickly.

"Thanks!" she said, flashing a smile.

Kelsey heard the printer in the corner of the room ramping up with the print jobs from those already finished. Unfazed, Kelsey clicked back over the answers to check them.

Thirty seconds later, the woman spoke again. "Hey, there is no 'E!'"

"Oops," Kelsey said in a flat tone, not even bothering to look at her.

The girl muttered some rather colorful obscenities, but Kelsey didn't care. She had arrived at the print page.

Her mouse hovered over the print button as she listened to the cluster of people already gathered around the printer.

"There's no black ink!" someone whispered fiercely.

"All of these pages are blank!" a young man with glasses hissed, wrinkling the stack of printed pages.

A young woman dressed in a red business suit marched haughtily to the door. She turned the knob, but it wouldn't budge.

"It's locked!" she announced. Then she pounded on the door. "Hey, we're stuck in here and the printer is out of ink!"

A few others came to the door and joined her in pounding on it. "Let us out of here." Still others calmly walked over to the printer, having just sent their print job. When their blank results page printed out blank, just like everyone else's, they threw it down and joined the increasing mob at the door.

Kelsey clicked 'print' and waited for the notification. After about ten seconds, a window flashed up on the screen, announcing that the ink cartridge was low.

In this case, 'low' apparently meant bone dry.

Kelsey canceled the print job and went back to inspect the document. Seeing that it was just a simple black text screen announcing that her test had been successfully submitted, she quickly copied the entire page and pasted it into a word processing program. Then she highlighted it all, went up to the top of the screen, and clicked on the font color button.

Hmmm, Kelsey thought, *I think I feel like teal today.* She clicked on the bluish-green color, and then, once again, printed the document.

She waited. The printer revved up. The sound caught the attention of everyone in the room. Gradually, people stopped yelling and pounding on the door as the machine made it's mechanical noises in preparation to spit the document out.

Kelsey stood and walked casually to the printer. A paper emerged and she quickly picked it up, seeing the neat teal lettering announcing her completion. She folded the paper in half to ensure no curious eyes could invade, and then she walked to the other end of the room.

Her silent audience seemed to collectively hold its breath as Kelsey slipped the paper through the mail slot. The door immediately opened.

"Kelsey Johnson?" Garrett's voice called.

Like the parting of the Red Sea, Kelsey's fellow test-takers moved aside and watched with open mouths as she exited the door. However, her passing through the threshold seemed to break the spell, and everyone else immediately crowded the door to leave the room.

Voices called out, "Hey, what's going on?

"How did she…?"

"So what are we supposed to do now?"

Neither Kelsey nor Garrett turned back, but as they passed the receptionist, Kelsey heard Garrett apologize with a smile before continuing on. Kelsey heard the mob behind her descend on the poor receptionist, and she immediately understood the reason for Garrett's preemptive apology.

Garrett led her to a small room and indicated she should sit down in front of a single computer.

"One more test," he announced.

"You said that with the last test," Kelsey reminded him.

Garrett shrugged. "In your case, I lied. Get used to it."

He then walked out, leaving Kelsey to marvel at his wonderful bedside manner.

Sighing, she turned her attention to the computer and began the test.

The first question popped up on the screen.

'Did anyone attempt to cheat during any of the tests today?'

Startled, Kelsey quickly typed, 'yes.'

She was then asked to give a detailed description of each person who had cheated and give a report as to their actions. Besides the blonde who had asked for her help, Kelsey had noticed two other men unobtrusively looking at other's screens during the different tests. One of them presumably got up to get a Kleenex in order to give a better view to his wandering eye.

After providing descriptions, Kelsey was then asked to pick the individuals out of a lineup of pictures that was flashed on the screen.

Kelsey felt slightly unnerved. This had been unlike any test she had ever taken. But just when she thought the observation questions were over, another flashed on the screen.

'Give a detailed description of Garrett Matthews.'

Kelsey swallowed and quickly wrote a thorough description, including everything from estimated height and weight, to hair color, note of the small scar near his left eyebrow, and a color analysis of his eyes.

She clicked 'submit' and another question popped up.

'Based on your first impression and observation, provide a character analysis of Agent Garrett Matthews.'

Kelsey paused, thinking. Then she quickly typed up her thoughts, based on her complete gut reaction. She painted Garrett as confident to the point of being cocky. He struck her as a man who got the job done. She didn't think he would do anything openly illegal, but probably lived in the gray areas. Finally, she thought he was too good looking. He was very likely a ladies man and was not at all opposed to using that to his advantage.

One more submit button, and she reached an announcement that she was on the final question.

But out of every question Kelsey had tackled today, it was that last one that unnerved her the most:

'You seem to have paid close attention to Agent Matthews' eyes. Please pick his eyes out of the following photos.'

With a dry mouth, Kelsey clicked through the photos and, without a second thought, put a check next to the pair of gray eyes that resembled a moody thunderstorm.

This hadn't been a standardized test. There was someone on the other end of the line. It was as if the wizard behind the curtain was controlling things to specifically target Kelsey, and it rattled her.

The door opened, but it wasn't Garrett.

A bald man with glasses entered the room. With a friendly smile, he extended his hand to Kelsey. "Hello, Miss Johnson, I'm Andrews. If you will follow me, I'll explain to you what is going on and answer any questions you may have.

Kelsey followed him to a comfortable office. Kelsey took a chair in front of the desk, while he positioned himself behind.

"Who are you, Mr. Andrews?" Kelsey immediately asked. She was tired of jumping through hoops. She wanted to know who she was dealing with and the reason behind the bizarre testing.

"I'm head of a Homeland Security division, and if you accept my offer, I will also be your boss."

"Offer?"

"Yes, Miss Johnson. I'm here to offer you a job as an agent with Homeland Security."

"Why?"

"Besides the fact that you passed our tests with flying colors? We've had our eye on you for a while. You may think you were handed a card at a job fair randomly, but you weren't. You were chosen specifically.

"But why? I don't have the best resume for this sort of thing."

"When you were graduating high school, your intentions were to join the military, were they not?"

Kelsey nodded hesitantly.

"The tests you were given at the time indicated you might be a good fit for Homeland Security. Tell me, Miss Johnson, exactly why did you not join the military?"

Kelsey met his eyes steadily, refusing to flinch. "If you already know so much about me, I'm willing to bet you already know the answer to that question. But if you want to hear me say it, then fine. After a psych evaluation, the military turned me down. The official conclusion was that events in my past could pose significant psychological issues that could prove risky in dangerous situations. And I would think that same reason should preclude me from being an agent in your organization. I'm sure you already know all about my rather colorful past. The curious thing is, if you already know all of that, why am I still here?"

Andrews waved his hand, as if swatting an annoying fly. "Not a concern. You will have a psych evaluation as standard protocol, but the results of that won't prevent you from having a job with us. I can use your skills, no matter what. Your IQ is high, your computer ability top-notch, and your observation skills, especially concerning Garrett Matthews eyes, are very impressive.

Andrews peered at her, almost challenging her to blush.

She did not.

He leaned forward. "I don't care what a psychologist said, no one needs to know about your history or your personal medical reports. I will seal those documents, and no one but I will have access. I need out-of-the-box thinkers who change the color of the ink when the black is out."

Twenty minutes later, Kelsey walked past the receptionist in possession of a new job. She had orders to report tomorrow, where she would be briefed on her training and the program that would pay for her to complete her degree. She had already signed contracts, but instead of being nervous about the commitment she had just made, she felt like she'd been thrown a rope to a new life. Her past would not define her. She would graduate college, be successful, and make a difference in this world.

With head held high, Kelsey walked to the glass doors at the front of the office building. Her gaze caught on a couple standing together to the left of the revolving door. A blonde in a mini skirt was smiling up at Garrett Matthews. Kelsey recognized her as the same blonde who had tried to cheat during the test. Garrett's head was bent toward the woman, and he was obviously flirting to the tune of the blonde's tinkling laughter.

As she passed, Garrett looked up. The instant their gazes locked, his eyes became completely flat, just as they had before. They lost all spark and became completely devoid of life.

A smile returned to his face only when he looked back down at the woman tugging on his arm.

And that was the exact moment when she disliked Garrett Matthews.

"I didn't hate you at first," Kelsey heard her own audible voice, and it startled her awake.

Instead of walking out the door to the office building and leaving Garrett Matthews behind, she was stuck in a box with the man and on the run from the U.S. government.

She realized she'd been lost in memories, a light sleep clouding her senses. Now she breathed deeply, waiting and hoping her voice hadn't awakened Garrett.

"What did I do wrong?" his voice rasped loudly in the silent box.

Kelsey swallowed, letting the pause lengthen with awkward silence until she could stand it no longer. Finally, she admitted, "You went through every woman I knew, ending with my best friend."

"Every woman but you."

Kelsey ignored his comment, denying that his words held any sting. Instead, she quietly spoke, unable to hide her resentment. "I disliked you because you disliked me first."

Garrett was silent. Thankfully, he didn't deny the truth, and as the quiet lengthened, she knew he wouldn't respond. Part of her longed to know why he had disliked her on sight that first day, but she didn't want to know if the truth would hurt. Knowing wouldn't change the current situation

Despite how they felt, they would need to work together. It seemed that all she could hope to have in common with Garrett was their mutual dislike, and for now, she hoped that emotion, negative as it was, would provide enough camaraderie to keep them alive.

Chapter 6

Kelsey snapped awake at the metallic screech of the trailer door sliding open. Garrett immediately placed his hand over hers in a calming gesture. As if she would utter a sound! Still, she couldn't bring herself to shrug off the warm pressure of his hand on hers.

Kelsey and Garrett had managed to remain undetected when the trailer had been loaded early that morning. With the steady rumble of the truck traveling to their unknown destination, Kelsey had finally been lulled into a dreamless sleep, only to be startled awake once again.

Voices echoed through the metal cavern as the men stepped into the trailer. While the men unloaded the cargo, Kelsey held her breath. Loading the trailer hadn't been nearly so nerve-racking, but would they really be content to leave two boxes in an otherwise empty trailer?

Though it was still pitch black in the box, she looked down at where Garrett's skin touched hers, as if she could somehow see the connection she felt. The hand on hers seemed almost comforting, and she couldn't part with it while knowing they could be discovered at any minute.

They waited, completely motionless, listening to the grunts of the men unloading the heavy shipment. She heard the shuffling footsteps get closer, and she felt the skin under Garrett's hand begin to perspire. She focused on slow, steady breathing. Footsteps stopped right outside their box.

"Hey, Jim!" a voice called loudly. "It looks like we got a couple of the wrong boxes. Judging by the addresses, these two aren't even supposed to go through this distribution center."

"Oh, that's right," a more muffled voice responded. "Tom said to leave those two alone. I think he already knew that they were in the wrong truck. He'll take care of it later."

"Good," the man said, his voice muting as he turned and walked back down the length of the trailer. "Those are some massive boxes. I don't want to be the one to move them, even if we did use one of the machines."

"Yeah, probably have some kind of dinosaur boxed up in there," they could hear Jim joke. "I'd hate to pay the shipping costs on that!"

Metal screeched again as the door rolled shut.

Ten seconds after the men's voices completely faded away, and Kelsey's breath came out in a whoosh. "What now?"

"We wait," Garrett replied.

Though Kelsey couldn't see him, his bored tone suggested his eyes were closed, and he was fully intending to nap.

The minutes wore on, and Garrett offered no further explanation. How long were they supposed to stay in this box? Kelsey really wanted to grill him for answers, but managed to keep quiet. Her legs were cramping, desperate to be stretched out, yet she wouldn't give Garrett the satisfaction of knowing that she was uncomfortable. If he could sit here relaxed in a cramped box for an infinite amount of time, then so could she.

Garrett seemed to be just waiting for her to crack.

Kelsey didn't know if her little quiet game was real or imagined, but the competitive edge was the only thing that kept her from angrily shoving Garrett out of the box until he answered her questions.

Everything was silent for what seemed like a very long time. Then abruptly, a door slammed and the truck started. Once again, they moved down a road.

Garrett wasn't alarmed, so Kelsey could only assume this was part of the plan, though he gave no explanation.

Not five minutes later, the truck slowed to a halt.

The sudden boom of cardboard breaking was followed by the flicker of Garrett's phone flashlight.

"This is our stop," Garrett announced, finally breaking his silence and crawling out of the box.

Kelsey followed, forgetting any attempt at grace in her eagerness to be out of the cardboard prison. She stumbled to her feet, her muscles stiff and sore. Reaching above her head, she stood on her tiptoes, trying to stretch every muscle in her body to end the protest.

"You must have a really good friend." Kelsey said, finally turning to where Garrett worked to extract the motorcycle from its box. "I assume this last driver took us to a place where we won't be seen when exiting."

Garrett nodded. "He's not a friend as much as a guy who owes me a lot of favors."

"Oh, really?" Kelsey asked, wondering how Garrett got someone to take such a big risk to help. "What kind of favors?"

"Well, it's kind of a favor for not turning him in," Garrett clarified with a somewhat sheepish smile. "I guess I'm what you call intuitive. I study people, and sometimes I get a feeling about what they are up to—their sins, so to speak. I am usually right. Now, I'm not so good at gathering evidence, but these people don't know that. Since I know certain secrets they would rather keep under wraps, they are quite helpful if I have a situation that requires assistance. And, of course, they are quite willing to help when I need certain favors, like a ride.

"I think the technical term for that is 'blackmail,'" Kelsey pointed out dryly.

"Not really," Garrett said, not seeming the least perturbed by her accusation. "No money ever changes hands. I don't actually have anything on them; they just don't know that. It's not blackmail, it's bluffing."

Kelsey felt nervous when Garrett opened the back of the truck. But the loud screech of metal didn't seem to raise any attention. In fact, the entire area seemed deserted. While it was broad daylight, the truck was parked in an alley between warehouses and contained no visible signs of life.

With Kelsey's help, Garrett got the motorcycle down the ramp and out of the truck. He then replaced the license plate with yet another different one and handed Kelsey the dorky helmet.

"So where are we going now?" Kelsey asked, obediently strapping the helmet on. She knew there was no chance Garrett would let her drive anyway. She might as well acquiesce this one time. Even though they weren't being followed now, they were still being hunted. Danger would be eminent until they found Garrett's safe house, and even then, there would likely be no such thing as safety until they found some evidence against the vice president.

"I have a... 'friend' who has a hunting lodge," Garrett finally answered. "We're headed up there."

By Garrett's tone of voice, it was obvious that this "friend" was of the same variety as the shipping truck "friend."

"I guess getting on your bad side is not a good thing, at least from your 'friends' perspective," Kelsey said, once again climbing on the motorcycle behind Garrett.

"I don't know, you've managed to be on my bad side pretty well for the last few years."

"True," Kelsey said, strangely grateful that he was at least admitting that he didn't like her. Honesty was better than veiled dislike. "But you don't have any dirt on me."

"Not yet."

With those two little words, fear rippled through her with the same ferocious energy of the motorcycle's engine roaring to life.

Garrett stepped on the gas, shooting out of the alley while Kelsey clung to his suit jacket. Taking back roads, Garrett navigated past the marks of civilization until they were winding up mountain roads. The pavement narrowed and trees formed a canopy overhead, blocking the warmth of the sun. Kelsey shivered, but refused to lean closer to Garrett. Instead, she sat as if she had a rod in her spine and gripped Garrett's jacket, not wanting to even feel the warm pressure of his body.

The beauty of the mountain scenery was mostly lost on Kelsey. She imagined horrible things about this hunting lodge safe house of Garrett's. Kelsey's life had never been cliché, but she'd seen enough movies to know that the attractive single man being forced to stay with the single woman in a remote, romantic hunting lodge was a recipe for a lot of things that Kelsey wished to avoid.

The only thing that gave her hope was the fact that they both intensely disliked each other. Kelsey realized that the real potential problem was with herself. For as much as she hated Garrett, she was reluctantly, irreversibly attracted to him, which made the thought of being trapped in an isolated, romantic mountain getaway both terrifying and alarmingly alluring.

The sound of the tires leaving the pavement startled Kelsey from her thoughts. Garrett slowed to compensate for the narrow dirt road.

At first the dust had been choking. But Garrett had found the right speed so the dirt plumed behind them. Kelsey shot a glance behind them. Through the dust, she confirmed that they still weren't being followed.

Kelsey couldn't deny that it really was beautiful up here. As they climbed in elevation, the sky seemed to get bluer as it peeked between the trees. It was still Spring, and Kelsey could smell dirt and pine and growing things all mixed together in a fresh, clean aroma that made one feel as if they'd never had a good breath of air before.

As a city girl, Kelsey didn't have a lot of experience in the mountains. Though the Ozarks were not quite what she had experienced in Rachel's Montana, they were enough to make the city girl long for a life more than skyscrapers and perfectly-landscaped parks.

She thought they must be getting close to the hunting lodge, but after another fifteen minutes winding up a steep strip of dirt, Kelsey wondered if they would ever arrive. This wasn't just a little remote. They hadn't passed another vehicle or seen another person since they left the paved road.

Garrett finally turned right. With the overgrown brush and trees, she didn't think that the path they were on could even be considered a road.

The dirt faded away completely, but Garrett kept going along a line of compact vegetation and hard ground that, with enough imagination, you could term a trail. One more sharp turn, and Garrett parked the motorcycle in the awning of the 'hunting lodge.'

But it wasn't a hunting lodge like any Kelsey had seen or even imagined.

It was a shack.

Nestled in the trees, it looked as if it had been assembled with wood scraps. Maybe the wood was just weathered and old, but it reminded Kelsey of something they might term a 'shanty.' The roof came to an off-centered peak and was made of what looked like dull scrap metal. The whole structure looked like it would collapse in complete exhaustion if encountered by the big bad wolf.

Kelsey knew her mouth was hanging open as she slid off the bike. "This wasn't quite what I was picturing when you said we were going to a hunting lodge."

Garrett shrugged. "We should be safe. No one is here this time of year. We're just fortunate it isn't hunting season. This place gets packed."

"Packed with what? Two people?" Kelsey asked. "Are you sure an adult can fit in that thing?"

Garrett smirked, looking up and down her small stature. "I'm not sure about an adult, but you should fit just fine."

Kelsey grimaced. She'd walked right into that one.

Ignoring him, she looked worriedly at the structure while Garrett unloaded his supplies from the side bags on the motorcycle. "Is there... water... and a restroom?"

"Oh, sure!" Garrett assured. "Come on. I'll give you the grand tour, and then we can talk about how we can beat the bad guy."

Kelsey followed Garrett as he took out an old key and unlocked the front door. With a loud, protesting screech, it opened. The dust of the unused interior filled Kelsey's sinuses, making her nose itch.

Though it wasn't dark, the tree canopy overhead made it dim inside the little shanty. Kelsey looked for a light switch, but found none.

"Electricity?" She asked, though she already knew the obvious answer.

"No," Garrett affirmed. "Don't need it. The stove runs on propane, and there are oil lamps, flashlights, and lanterns fully stocked."

At least there was a stove. There had been a few seconds where Kelsey had visions of trying to warm up soup in the large stone fireplace that dominated one end of the room.

Kelsey looked around, noting the placement of the stove at the opposite end of the room. Several chairs and couches sat clustered around the fireplace. Rugs dotted the hardwood floor, and the walls actually looked nice with the natural, rustic wood.

All-in-all, the interior was much nicer than the exterior. The large windows looking out at the trees from the wall opposite the front door were definitely the most appealing feature. But there was something missing. It was all one open room. Kelsey counted two doors—the front and the back. Where were the bedrooms?

Then Kelsey spotted several cots stacked together in the corner. No bedrooms, or maybe just one large one that also happened to be the kitchen, living room, and dining room. But something else was missing too,

"So here it is!" Garrett said brightly turning a full circle while his arms spread wide, gesturing to the whole room. "Now you've had the full tour."

"Restroom?" Kelsey asked pointedly.

"Out back." Garrett said, using his thumb to point behind him.

And most aggravating, he said it with a straight face.

"I thought you said there was a restroom!" she accused.

"There is!" he insisted, wide-eyed and offended. "There's an outhouse out back."

"An outhouse doesn't qualify as a restroom!"

"Well, excuse me! Here I thought you could handle anything. I thought you were tough and had the 'anything-you-can-do-I-can-do-better' attitude!"

"I do! I mean, I am. I mean… outhouses don't count!" And with that, Kelsey marched out the back and slammed the door, on her way to become acquainted with the stinky miniature shack that served the larger one.

*****

Exactly six minutes later, Kelsey walked back in to see Garrett hang up one of his burner phones, a frown on his face.

"So what's the plan?" Kelsey asked, not wanting to beat around the bush. Thankfully, the outhouse had been equipped with some waterless antibacterial soap, but it hadn't quite been enough to wash her entire body in. Kelsey didn't consider herself a neat freak, but outhouses apparently brought to light ever natural germophobe tendency she had.

The faster they developed a plan, the faster they acquired evidence against the vice president, the faster they got out of here. One time in the outhouse had been enough.

Garrett tossed the phone on a little end table and flopped on a cushy, worn, leather couch with his hands up and supporting behind his head. "I tried to call Dawson, but he didn't answer, which isn't a good sign. Maybe they've gotten to him already. I was counting on his help."

"Dawson doesn't know anything about the case, though, right?" Kelsey asked, not daring to hope that someone on the outside would have useful knowledge.

"No, he only knows what you knew—that I was investigating the political angle of the terrorist ring. "But Dawson is one of the few I can trust. Even if everyone, including all of Homeland Security, paints me as a traitor, Dawson won't believe it. He would risk everything to help me."

"I guess I hadn't realized you two were that close, especially since you tried to steal Dawson's girl," Kelsey said, making no attempt at subtlety.

"Rachel chose him," he said with a simple shrug. "End of story. You're right in that haven't always liked Dawson. But he's kind of grown on me the last year or so. I know that even if the man didn't like me, or consider me a friend, he would still do what was right, because it's right.

"Friend?" Kelsey questioned, her eyebrows raised, silently asking if his use of the term resembled his previous "friends."

Garrett shook his head. "If Dawson had any dirt, I would take it to my grave. He and Rachel are just about the only true friends I have."

"You can't really mean that!" Kelsey said, ignoring the pull of sympathy at his words. "Even if Dawson isn't available, don't you have other friends you can take advantage of?"

At Garrett's silent glare, Kelsey continued, trying to deliberately back off on her tone. Though Garrett grated on her nerves, getting into another argument wouldn't get them closer to getting out of here. "Maybe instead of a friend, you have a contact. That source who died couldn't have been the only one. Someone you've met has to know something. If we know who to put pressure on, maybe we can get a message to Andrews, or Dawson and Rach—"

"There is no one," Garrett said, cutting her off with a wave of his hand, as if dismissing her suggestion like it was an annoying fly.

Kelsey lost her patience, completely giving up on the idea of trying to maintain the peace. "So you're telling me you've had a year and none of your romantic entanglements include a woman who can get us any information or help."

Garrett groaned, leaning his head back. "Give it a rest, Johnson! I know I dated a lot of women, which you apparently took offense at. But I'm not that guy anymore."

"Oh, really," Kelsey said, folding her arms across her chest and raising her eyebrows skeptically. "I don't believe it. People don't change that much. Exactly how many women have you gone through this year, trying to collect 'evidence?'"

Garrett suddenly stood from the couch and turned to face Kelsey, his eyes blazing with fierce sparks. "You haven't been around me at all since Miami over a year ago. You don't know me, or know what I've been through. You don't believe in

God, do you? Well, I do. I know I didn't act like it, but I was raised a Christian, and in the past year, I've gone back to my faith. I won't pretend it's easy, but I do know I'm not the same man you hated that first day."

Silence stretched between them. Finally, Kelsey looked away first, breaking the intensity. "Look, I'm sorry, but it's a little difficult for me to believe all of that when I watched you go through every woman in Homeland Security."

"Every woman except you."

Kelsey couldn't meet his gaze. This was the second time he'd mentioned this fact, and it smarted just as it had the first time. He had never even tried with her. Never flirted, never even feigned interest. Not even once. "Yes, everyone but me," Kelsey admitted, working to keep all emotion out of her tone and bravely raising her eyes to once again meet his.

"So tell me, Johnson, is the problem that I was romantically involved with so many women, or that you were not one of them?"

Chapter 7

Kelsey glared at Garrett, not allowing him to see the sting of truth in his words.

"Tell me about the case," she gritted out.

Garrett's eyebrows lifted in mock amusement. "So we're changing the subject now, are we? What's wrong, Johnson? Things get a little too personal?

"The case," Kelsey repeated, once again folding her arms across her front as if completely willing to wait.

"I already told you everything," Garrett replied, stubbornly folding his arms to match hers.

"Start at the beginning," Kelsey instructed. "You must have missed someone or something."

Garrett sighed, flopping back on the couch and running a hand through his hair wearily before responding. "I really think you already know it all, Johnson. After Phillip Saunders was apprehended, certain evidence indicated the possibility that he was not the highest up in the terrorist organization—that there may be a political angle."

Kelsey nodded. "I remember Rachel being concerned about that. She said Phillip ranted about being a patriot and how he'd been offered an unimaginable amount of money."

"Good memory," Garrett acknowledged. "You would have thought with that kind of evidence, a trail would have been easier to find. We tracked Phillip's bank accounts and his movements for at least two years prior to his arrest, and yet nothing led to any evidence beyond those initial rants. Everyone thought it was a dead end. Then I found my informant. And now he's dead, and we're back to a dead end."

"So your entire investigation began with Phillip's own admissions," Kelsey mused, walking to the large windows. She looked out, observing the forest as if it was a picture, yet lost deep in thought.

"Yes," Garrett supplied. "Without Phillip, we had nothing. And even with Phillip, we had nothing more than the ramblings of a domestic terrorist. It isn't as if that kind of crazy can be trusted in any way."

Kelsey didn't respond for several minutes.

Thankfully, Garrett gave her space and began inspecting every crevice in the shanty, taking stock of what supplies were available.

"Let me see a burner phone," Kelsey ordered, finally turning from the window.

Garrett looked at her questioningly, even as he handed her the requested item.

"I have a plan," she said vaguely, dialing a number before Garrett could question her further.

"Hello, this is Snow White. We have a poisoned apple situation." Kelsey hung up the phone.

"What was that?" Garrett asked.

"I just called Rachel."

"But you hung up.

"She'll call me back on a secure line."

"She can't do that! If you called her on her regular phone. Homeland Security will have record of it. That's why it's a burner phone. You use and toss it!"

Kelsey started to respond, but the sound of a phone ringing interrupted her. "I'm not an idiot," she said, reaching into her jacket and pulling out a small phone. "You have multiple burner phones, but I only need one."

She pressed the answer button.

"Kelsey, did you try on the dress?" Rachel asked eagerly. "Does it fit? Do you like it? I don't quite know if it's the right yellow, but I—"

"Rachel, it's a poisoned apple situation. I haven't exactly had time to try on the bridesmaid dress you sent."

"Oh, right. But with the wedding so close and you the maid of honor, I kind of need to know!"

"I'm sure it's fine, Rachel, but it's in New York, and I'm well... I don't know where I am. But bad guys are trying to kill us."

"Right. Poisoned apple. Are you and Garrett safe?" Rachel asked, swiftly turning to business.

By her mention of Garrett, Kelsey realized Rachel likely already knew of the situation they were in. But chances were, Rachel had heard the version where they shot at government agents and ran off.

"Yes, we are fine. But I need your help getting into a prison."

"Phillip?"

"Yes," Kelsey answered.

Rachel was one of the smartest people Kelsey knew. She had very likely already surmised most of Kelsey and Garrett's current situation.

After thinking about it, Kelsey had concluded that the only way to end this thing was to go back to their original source of information. But to do that, she needed Rachel's help. "I need to talk to your brother."

"If you give me a few details on what info you're looking for, I can pay him a visit and try to get it out of him," Rachel volunteered. "Pressure is really hot right now. Everyone is looking for the two of you."

"I know that would be the safer option, but I need to be the one to speak with Phillip in person."

There was silence on the other end of the line for the space of several seconds.

"Then I guess we need to break into a prison."

The next two minutes were spent outlining a plan with as few words as possible. Though she knew Garrett was carefully watching and listening, she doubted he would be able to completely follow the conversation, with the code words she and Rachel were throwing around.

"So we'll meet you and Uncle Henry tomorrow morning at the fishing pond," Kelsey clarified. "See you then."

Kelsey lifted the phone off her ear to hang it up.

"Kelsey, have you told him?"

Rachel's soft question made her pause.

"No." Kelsey didn't need to think to know exactly what Rachel was referring.

"You need to tell him," Rachel said kindly. "I know it's hard, but Kelsey he needs to know. With the situation you're in... Kelsey, please tell him."

"I'll think about it."

"What about the dreams, Kelsey?"

Kelsey swallowed. Those wouldn't happen. "I'm fine, Rachel. I said I'd think about it."

But she didn't want to think about it. Though she knew Rachel was suggesting that their safety might be compromised because of Kelsey's past, she didn't want to tell Garrett. That was personal. And something she'd worked hard to forget and overcome. If only it didn't keep following her. Rachel was one of two people who knew her secret. And she would prefer to keep it that way.

Kelsey hung up and turned to Garrett. "I have GPS coordinates of where to meet Rachel and Dawson tomorrow morning. They are going to help me get in to see Phillip Saunders."

"Why Phillip? Don't you think he's already been questioned by professional interrogators? The man won't budge."

"He doesn't need to budge," Kelsey clarified. "He just needs to tell me where he hid the evidence."

"What evidence?"

Kelsey wearily sat down on the couch for the first time. The night was catching up to her, and though she was extremely hungry, right now, exhaustion was winning. "A man like Phillip keeps evidence," Kelsey said, wishing she didn't have to explain the details to Garrett. "The fact that he's still alive tells me that he has something on the vice president. It's his insurance policy."

"Nice theory," Gaett quipped, as if completely dismissing Kelsey's idea. "But Phillip is in a maximum security federal prison. Even if we weren't wanted by every government agency, you would have trouble getting in if you weren't family or legal counsel. Besides, even if you get in, all visits are recorded."

Kelsey rolled her eyes. "And you're an agent? I thought you didn't say something was impossible, you figured out how to make it possible. Don't worry. Rachel will take care of the details."

"If Rachel and Dawson help us, they're putting their lives at risk as well." Garrett sat on the arm of a recliner, clearly prepared to continue criticism of Kelsey's plan.

"That's not a problem they are unfamiliar with," Kelsey said, getting up to scrounge for food. Maybe if Dawson had a little distraction, he would give the interrogation a rest. With her back to him, she couldn't resist flinging back, "Besides, you were going to do the same thing. You tried to call Dawson."

Garrett followed. "Yes, but I didn't get through. How was it that I couldn't reach Dawson, but you could reach Rachel? And who is Snow White?"

Kelsey mimicked a curtsy. "I am Snow White. At least, according to Rachel. Rachel has this habit of nicknaming people. You know how she calls Dawson, 'Hollywood.' She calls me 'Snow White.' She claims I look like her, I guess. With our work being so dangerous, we decided it would be a good idea to develop an emergency plan just between us. We wanted the other person to be a failsafe so that nothing could happen to us like what happened when Dawson was kidnapped. So we have a system of codes that probably sound like ridiculous gibberish to someone listening, but have meaning to us. Of course, 'poisoned apple' means that the other person's life is in danger."

Kelsey found a can of chili and checked the expiration date. Seeing that it was still good, she handed it to Garrett.

While still speaking, he opened the can and plopped the contents into a pot on the stove. "So, at the mention of the code words, Rachel knew to call you back using a secured line, at a pre-arranged burner number?"

"Yes," Kelsey searched the cupboards and drawers for bowls and spoons. "We have an app that allows us to assign multiple burner numbers to a phone. Then, when one is used, we delete it. Rachel and I have five usable burner numbers memorized. Well, four now. All the numbers are attached to a single phone—one not associated with Homeland Security." Kelsey held up the plain, black phone and tweaked it back and forth for emphasis. "This one."

"So, if you have a burner phone capable of producing multiple numbers, then why did you waste one of mine?" Garrett asked, offended.

Kelsey shrugged. "If I would have taken out a phone and tried to call, especially after you chucked my other one, you would have freaked out. So I decided to play the game your way. But at my message, Rachel knew how to respond. I knew she would call me on one of the secure numbers, then we would dispose of the number. Sorry to waste your phone. Well, I'm not really sorry. I was trying to humor you."

"Yeah, right," Garrett shot back dryly. He stirred the chili, found a package of crackers in another cupboard, and tossed them to Kelsey. "So, tomorrow morning? I guess the only thing to do until then is wait."

Kelsey was silent. At least Garrett finally seemed willing to accept her plan, but now the larger problem surfaced in her mind. How would she get through the rest of the day, and then the night, alone in a small shack with Garrett?

Garrett shut off the stove, spooned some chili into a bowl, and handed it to Kelsey.

"Hey," he said suddenly. "You said Rachel had a nickname for everyone. Does she have one for me?"

"Yes," Kelsey said simply. "Pretty much everyone we work with has a nickname in Rachel's world. I think she has an 'Ahab.' She calls Holmes, 'Dilbert.' You know that blonde from accounting? I think you went out with her for a while. She's 'Barbie.' None of her names are unkind, but she also doesn't publicize them."

"What's my name?" Garrett asked again.

Kelsey quickly spooned the hot chili into her mouth. Pointing that she couldn't speak, she turned her back on him and headed back to the couch.

"You're not going to tell me?" Garrett asked, clearly insulted.

"It isn't my business to tell," Kelsey said in between bites. "Ask Rachel yourself."

"That bad, huh?" Garrett said, as if trying to decide if he really wanted to know after all.

Kelsey busily stuffed crackers into her mouth. There was no way she was going to tell Garrett his nickname. The man certainly didn't need anything else to add to his already swollen ego!

Content with silence, Snow White concentrated on her food, trying to muster the courage to face hours alone with a man she couldn't decide if she hated or not.

And it was the "or not" part that scared her most.

Chapter 8

Kelsey lay awake long after Garrett's breathing evened out on the cot across the room. She should be completely exhausted, and yet her eyes were wide open, watching the flames in the fireplace.

Garrett had prayed over the soup. That bothered her. Strange that with as much danger they were in, as many arguments they'd had over the past twenty-four hours, that simple prayer is what bothered her most.

They had actually gotten along pretty well this evening, keeping the discussion mostly to the case and possible scenarios for breaking into the prison, securing evidence, and getting out of this mess. They took turns periodically going outside, scouting for signs of their enemies, but both were fairly certain they were safe for now. But tomorrow would be different. They would have to leave the little shack with the outhouse and try to clear their names, while avoiding getting killed in the process.

Night had descended early, the trees' shadows getting deeper, longer, and melding together to form a close darkness that made Kelsey feel safe and yet nervous at the same time. The mountain air was cold without the sun, and Garrett built a fire in the fireplace while Kelsey set up the cots and blankets on opposite sides of the room.

At some point, Garrett had located a couple sets of clothes for them to change into. Garrett got the better end of the deal, however. While he was much more comfortable than in his suit, the clothes provided for Kelsey were about 10 times too big for her petite frame. Hoping that Rachel remembered to bring some spare clothes tomorrow, Kelsey had tucked herself in bed, not even saying a word when Garrett returned to climb into his own cot. Within minutes, his deep breathing filled the quiet room.

Kelsey thought about giving up on sleep and playing the role of sentry for a few hours. But she and Garrett had both agreed that they were as safe as possible, and a good night's sleep was more important for both of them than unnecessary security measures. Yet, even though she tried to distract herself with other things, her mind kept drifting back to Garrett's prayer.

Fine! She told herself in frustration. It was just a prayer. *Why does it bother you so much?*

Kelsey and God had parted ways long ago, if they'd ever been together to begin with. She knew the story of Jesus, and had heard the gospel message enough to preach it herself. It wasn't as if she didn't think Christianity plausible. It was more that she didn't think she needed to care for God when he obviously didn't care for her.

If Garrett was a Christian, then God must like him, which just exacerbated the difference. Kelsey had heard Jews referred to as God's "chosen people." By definition, Christians were God's people as well. Didn't that make them "chosen," too?

So why had God chosen Garrett and not her? She knew Garrett's life hadn't been paved with candy canes, but he obviously felt God's existence and love enough to be one of the chosen.

Yet Kelsey had long concluded that if God existed, and if He loved her, then there would have been no way He would have allowed January 23rd.

Kelsey continued to watch the flames, letting them almost hypnotize her into a shallow sleep. She still saw the flames, and yet, they morphed into figures that were fighting. The larger flame pushed the smaller one. The smaller one cowered, raising its arms for protection, yet the larger one kept coming after it, kicking, hitting, showing no mercy.

Then Kelsey, once again, heard the familiar screams. The man yelling obscenities over and over, while the woman cried, begging him to stop.

"Dad, please!" Kelsey cried, rushing forward. "Stop!"

Kelsey grabbed at his arm, trying to snap him out of the drunken rage.

But instead of giving him pause, Kelsey's intervention increased his fury. He took the hand at his elbow and grabbed it. Then, grabbing her other arm as well, he picked her up. In that split second, Kelsey saw his eyes, and felt fear like she'd never known before. She no longer recognized him. Her father's eyes were fogged over with cold, violent rage. There was no reason, no hint of humanity left.

Then he threw her.

She hit the wall, feeling her left arm snap beneath her.

"Jerry, no!" her mom gasped, pulling herself up to defend her daughter.

But he kicked her back down, continuing the beating.

He was going to kill her mom. There was no way anyone could live through that kind of beating.

Kelsey picked herself up and rushed to her parents' room. She opened her dad's drawer and pulled out his gun. Then she retrieved the cordless phone on their night stand. With her hurt left arm hanging limply at her side, she tucked the gun under her right arm and used her hand to hold the phone. She dialed 911with shaking fingers, all while her feet propelled her back to the living room.

With the number dialed, Kelsey tucked the phone between her cheek and her shoulder and took out the gun.

"911. What is your emergency?'

"My dad won't stop beating my mom. He's going to kill her!"

"What is your location?"

But Kelsey couldn't speak. At the sight of her mom, the phone dropped.

Her face was covered in blood. Her eyes were closed, and yet the room was still filled with her father's screams, the violence continuing.

If the police came, they would be too late.

Her mom whimpered, curling up in a ball in the corner.

Kelsey lifted the gun.

"Dad, stop! Please stop!" she begged, tears streaming down her face. Then she screamed. "Dad, stop!"

He paid no attention to her. His foot lifted to crush her mother one last time.

With a cry of agony, Kelsey pulled the trigger. Twice.

She didn't shut her eyes. Instead, she watched his body jerk with the impact of two bullets in the back. She saw him freeze, and then, as if in slow motion, he crumpled to the floor.

Sobbing, Kelsey rushed to him, turning him over to see open, lifeless eyes no longer filled with rage.

Unable to stand, Kelsey crawled over to where she left the phone, then crawled back to her mother. With her good arm, she pulled her mom's head into her lap and smoothed the blood-caked hair away from her face.

Sobbing so hard she couldn't breathe, she put the phone to her ear.

"Please help me!" she sobbed. "I… just… killed my dad."

"Kelsey! Kelsey, wake up!"

Someone gently shook her. She felt hands running over her face and hair.

"Kelsey, come on! Wake up! It's just a dream. You're safe!"

She heard sobbing, then realized the sound came from her own raw throat.

She opened her eyes to find Garrett bending over her with his brow furrowed in concern, his arms cradling her.

Kelsey sat bolt upright, running her hands over her tear-soaked cheeks and through her sweat-dampened hair. "I'm sorry," she whispered, her voice hoarse. "I had a... bad dream."

Without a single question, Garrett wordlessly picked her up, carried her the few short steps to the couch, and sat down with her secure in his arms.

Kelsey sat stiffly for several moments, but Garrett kept gentle yet firm hold of her while his strong fingers smoothed her hair. At the warm comfort of his embrace, tears eventually began to fall. But instead of the violent sobs of before these were the soft tears of deep grief and loneliness.

Garrett held her without saying a word. His arms stayed strong, safe, and comforting until the last tear trailed down her face and her eyes closed in peaceful sleep. And still he stayed.

Chapter 9

"Since you don't want to talk about anything else, can you at least tell me where we're supposed to meet Dawson and Rachel?"

Kelsey sighed, continuing to walk forward through the brush. This had not been an ideal morning, and she certainly didn't need Garrett nagging her in an already stressful situation!

She had awoken this morning in the exact same position that she'd fallen asleep—in Garrett's arms. She had looked up to find Garrett's head tipped back and eyes closed. She tried to delicately extract herself, but the moment she moved, Garrett's eyes flipped open.

Kelsey scrambled from his lap, headed for the safety of the horrid outhouse, and refused to speak a word about what had happened.

At Garrett's gentle questioning concern, asking if she was okay, Kelsey had simply said she'd had a nightmare but was fine.

"Awkward" was too mild of a word to describe the tension that stretched taut between them. After a breakfast of something that Kelsey imagined was supposed to resemble oatmeal, they had packed their meager belongings and left on the motorcycle to meet Rachel and Dawson at the pre-arranged coordinates.

When they were close, Kelsey insisted that they park the motorcycle, hide it in some brush, and walk the rest of the way. Garrett was reluctant to part with the motorcycle, but finally agreed. They were supposed to meet their friends at a lake. The chances of encountering campers, fishermen, and others enjoying the lake was very high. And it might be difficult to be inconspicuous on a motorcycle that was likely wanted by the United States government.

"They are supposed to be here," Kelsey said, finally answering Dawson's question. "How close are we to the exact GPS coordinates? They will likely be standing on top of them."

"*We* are standing on top of them!" Garrett insisted, checking his handheld device. "All I see is that massive travel trailer parked at the campsite."

Kelsey laughed. "That must be Uncle Henry!"

"What are you talking about?" Garrett asked, his confusion clearly turning to frustration.

For a guy used to being in charge, Kelsey knew following someone else's plan was a difficult exercise for Garrett.

Kelsey explained. "'Uncle Henry' is a code word Rachel and I use to describe an extraction that requires a large vehicle, usually for storage. In our case, I knew we needed something to haul your motorcycle. When I mentioned 'Uncle Henry,' Rachel likely knew exactly what we needed it for, since I'm sure everyone in every government department is aware of what kind of escape vehicle we used. See the toy hauler at the back of that trailer? Your dad's motocycle should fit nicely in there."

"Why 'Uncle Henry'?" Garrett asked, his mouth creasing up in a reluctant smile.

"Rachel has an uncle named Henry. He travels the country in his massive, fully-equipped travel trailer. And she says that every time a newer, bigger one comes on the market, he trades up."

Garrett nodded. "Makes sense. But if that's Uncle Henry, where are Rachel and Dawson?"

They walked to the trailer, looking around. They were just getting ready to knock on the door, when the sound of several vehicles broke the silence of the peaceful lake. Startled, they looked up to see three black SUV's moving through the trees.

Kelsey and Garrett dove to the opposite side of the trailer. With the trailer's position, it provided a great barrier where they hopefully couldn't be seen from anyone on the other side. But they couldn't see either. Instead, they heard the vehicles park, and then the slamming of car doors.

"Anyone here?" someone called out.

"No, looks like a bust. The only people I see are an old couple fishing down at the lake."

"We'd better ask if they've seen our guys, just to be thorough."

As footsteps crunched down to the lake, Garrett snuck around to the front of the truck, which was still attached to the trailer.

"Where are you going?" Kelsey whispered. "We need to get out of here!"

"I'm not going to let Dawson and Rachel have all the fun!" Garrett whispered back.

Kelsey looked around. Had he spotted them? Though she didn't see anyone, Kelsey followed Garrett as he scrambled from tree to tree, in a crouched position, following the men they should have been avoiding. Kelsey counted six of them. From their standard, cookie-cutter suits, she guessed them to be FBI.

They stopped and Kelsey heard them greet the older couple. Though she couldn't get a good look at them with their backs to the trees, she saw gray hair and long poles, so she assumed they were fishing.

Garrett and Kelsey maneuvered around until the agents and the older couple were directly in front of them through the veil of lacy leaves.

"Have you seen this couple?" One of the suits asked, the pleasantries now over.

The woman leaned her head over. "I'm not sure," came her voice, thin and raspy. "I need my glasses to tell for sure."

The man moved close to give her a better look.

She shook her head. "What do you think, Woodrow?" she asked her husband.

"I may or may not have seen them," the old man growled. "It depends on who's asking."

One of the men on the end pulled something out. "Sir, we're the FBI. We're searching for these persons who are considered armed and dangerous. A lead suggested they may be in the area around this time."

The old man moved toward the man on the end, as if to examine the badge. "And are you all FBI?" he asked, clearly skeptical.

"Yes, sir, we are."

All of the men moved as if to produce their badges.

"I caught one! I caught one!" The old lady screeched suddenly.

Her pole jerked sharply as if to set the hook, smacking the agent behind her in the face.

At his yelp, Kelsey saw the old man move. But suddenly he didn't seem so old anymore.

The agent beside him dropped to the ground.

Garrett leapt from the brush, directly onto the back of the agent standing closest to the trees. Following suit, Kelsey stepped through the trees in time to see the old lady drop the agent who had encountered her fishing pole with a trademark Rachel Saunders' nerve strike to the neck.

Three shocked men turned to Kelsey. Immediate recognition dawned in their eyes, and one of them reached for his gun. The poor man was closest to Rachel, however, and Kelsey knew he would never make the draw. Not waiting, she took a step and dropped, swinging her leg in a swift kick of her heel to the back of the knee of the agent closest to her. Both his legs immediately collapsed, and he dropped to the ground.

She then rose, jumping in one smooth motion to plant a snap kick in the center of the other agent's chest. Knowing he'd be down and not able to breathe for a moment, she turned back to the other fallen agent. But the not-so-old man, Dawson, was already snapping a pair of cuffs onto him.

Kelsey pulled out her own pair of cuffs and snapped them onto the agent who lay gasping, flat on his back.

All the agents were down in an encounter that had taken less than twenty seconds from when Rachel had "caught the fish."

Garrett and Dawson drug their captives over to the two Kelsey had laid out. Then Dawson went to help Rachel haul over her two. Kelsey hadn't seen what Rachel had done to the man with the gun, but he was still unconscious as he was dragged over. And his arms were held, not with handcuffs, but with fishing line.

"I ran out of handcuffs," Rachel explained, "so I had to improvise. I hated to do it, though. That's nice fishing line."

"Good idea," Dawson said, then he and Garrett made quick work of tying up the feet of all of the agents with fishing line.

"Now what do we do with them?" Dawson asked. "Leave them or take them with us?"

"I say leave them," Kelsey answered. "Someone is going to be up to look for them before dark. But I think that will give us more time than if we take them and drop them somewhere. We can also make a call to let their buddies know where they are. None of them are injured worse than bruised pride and maybe a headache. They should be fine."

With everyone agreed, Rachel and Dawson gathered their gear and the foursome headed back to the trailer, leaving their captives with a nice view of the lake.

"Oh, I almost forgot!" Rachel said, returning to pull out a stringer of about five good-sized fish from where it had been tethered at the shore.

Once out of earshot of the FBI agents, Garrett turned to Dawson. "So, how many of those did you catch, Daws?" he asked, a devilish grin on his face.

"I've never been able to out-fish Rachel, and you know it," Dawson growled.

"I thought Carson was teaching you," Garrett asked innocently, referring to Rachel's dad.

"He did," Dawson said stiffly.

Garrett's muffled laughter could still be heard as he hurried to retrieve the motorcycle.

They were soon on their way, Dawson and Rachel in the front seat of the king cab truck, Garrett and Kelsey in the back, and the motorcycle loaded safely in the toy hauler at the back of the fifth wheel trailer.

"Do you think we were recognized?" Rachel asked, worry lining her voice. She pulled off the gray wig to let her long, blonde hair free, and then began working to remove the sagging plastic cheeks and makeup from her face.

"No," Dawson assured. "We don't know those FBI agents; I've never encountered them before. We were careful never to use our real names—"

"And your disguises were genius!" Garrett finished. "With that makeup, you two really did look old! Kelsey didn't even recognize you."

Kelsey rolled her eyes. She could always count on Garrett to throw her under the bus! Nobody would have recognized them with disguises on par with professional Hollywood stage costumes!

"I'm just grateful you guys came," Kelsey said. "I know those disguises were a lot of work, but you also risked your lives and careers to help us. And you did all of that without knowing any of the details of why we are on the run."

"You're our friends," Rachel assured, pausing in her makeup removal task. She turned around in her seat, looking at Garrett and Kelsey with sincere blue eyes still decorated with impressive crow's feet. "We know you well enough to be certain you don't work for the dark side. You need our help; we need to give it. No questions asked."

Dawson nodded, keeping his eyes straight ahead as he drove. "We may not know all the details, but we can make a few educated guesses. This is the same case that started over a year-and-a-half ago. Rachel's case. It's time the foul thing is dead and buried. Besides, there isn't much danger to us. We took precautions."

Rachel reached over to Dawson and yanked off one bushy gray eyebrow.

"Ouch!" He exclaimed. "Warn a guy, will you? I think you took off my real eyebrow with that fake one."

"Sorry!" Rachel exclaimed. "I didn't know it would hurt. They are supposed to be 'easy to remove.'"

"Well, that is obviously false advertising!" Dawson said, reaching one hand up to rub his brow.

"What do you mean, you 'took precautions?' Kelsey asked, drawing the conversation off Dawson's eyebrows and back to the case at hand.

"Even if we are suspected of helping you, it won't matter," Dawson said confidently. "We gave ourselves an alibi."

"So where are Dawson Tate and Rachel Saunders at this moment?" Kelsey asked curiously.

"They took a few days off for wedding preparations and flew to Montana," Rachel said, smiling. "Or rather, our cell phones and tracking devices did. My dad will pick up a box at the airport, drive it around a bit, and then send it back to New York via a flight attendant who is a family friend."

Kelsey shot an annoyed glance at Garrett, who wasn't participating at all in the conversation. Instead, he had picked up what looked like an iPad, and had his nose buried in it ever since.

Kelsey, still concerned, turned back to Rachel and Dawson. "But still, if someone is monitoring you carefully, it might look suspicious. It's pretty difficult for a box to imitate everyday human movements." She knew her friends were taking a huge risk by helping them, and she didn't want them to get caught. It was bad enough that she and Garrett were wanted and on the run. If it was discovered that they had even contacted Rachel and Dawson, then they would be in the same situation.

"Andrews will cover for us," Dawson assured. "If anyone asks our location, he'll show them the tracking proof that we are in Montana

"So you told Andrews about our plan?" Garrett said, looking up from the iPad.

Maybe he was listening to the conversation more than it appeared.

"No, we didn't," Dawson assured, "though I'm sure he suspected. He knew if you needed help, we were the ones you would contact. So he equipped us and is covering for us, all under the table, of course. He wouldn't want to know the details anyway. That way, he can honestly say he knows nothing. On the outside, he has to appear to be using all his assets to locate and bring you in."

"What exactly are you doing?" Kelsey asked Garrett, finally fed up as his all-consuming focus returned to the electronic tablet. What could be more important than their discussion?

"Research," Garrett answered simply.

"That's one of the devices Andrews gave me," Dawson said, looking at Garrett and Kelsey in the rearview mirror. "Not that I don't trust our boss, but I don't. I made sure it didn't have any tracking or recording devices. That one was obviously meant for Garrett. I tried to start it up and it required Garrett's fingerprint. I take that to mean Andrews was taking precautions and had some intel that maybe Garrett would understand."

"Do you care to share with the rest of the class?" Kelsey asked Garrett pointedly.

"Not really," he said, though he turned off the tablet and scooted forward in his seat. "Let's discuss the plan."

Why wasn't he looking at her? His eyes were straight ahead on Rachel and Dawson in the front seat, and there was a strange tension exuding from him, almost as if he was avoiding Kelsey in the seat beside him. What had been on that tablet?

"Since we had to leave some friends back there, we'll need to hurry straight to the prison before they send the cavalry after us," Dawson said, his eyes focused on the road. "We'll drop the trailer off to be a little less conspicuous. But that will be the easy part. Breaking into a federal prison is going to be the tricky part."

"But we have everything set up," Rachel clarified. "As long as everyone knows their part and everything goes according to plan, it should be quick and relatively painless."

Unfortunately, Kelsey knew that was easier said than done.

Over the next few minutes, Rachel outlined the plan, providing maps and instructing each person in their role. By the time Dawson pulled into an RV park, all the details were ironed out, and everyone knew their necessary tasks.

"I'm just not sure about the part where I have to impersonate Rachel," Kelsey said honestly. "I'm sure you've noticed that I am *significantly* lower on the elevation scale. You're a frequent visitor at the prison, Rachel. Surely someone will recognize you and notice that you've shrunk!"

"That's exactly why we've outlined the plan in such a specific way," Rachel assured. "We checked the duty lists for today, and I've never met the guard assigned to Phillip's area. Besides, give yourself a little credit. You're into details. By now, I'm sure you know all my little tics. You can probably pretend to be me better than I can!"

Though she appreciated Rachel's vote of confidence, she was still nervous.

It was a good plan, in a crazy, breaking-into-a-federal-prison sort of way. But Kelsey knew that no mission ever went perfectly. And with this one, she had the awful sense that if one single detail failed to execute, then the whole scheme would fall apart.

Then they would all suddenly find themselves inside a federal prison with no escape.

Chapter 10

Kelsey kept her head down as she swept, hoping the hat fully concealed her face.

Rachel walked into the restroom, right on time.

So far, so good. Everything was going according to plan, but this next step would be the most difficult.

After Dawson dropped off the trailer and paid for the spot at the RV park, they had come directly to the prison. Rachel had checked through security while Kelsey had donned the scrubs of a prison employee, presented false ID that matched a bogus profile previously inserted into the system by Rachel, and got to work cleaning.

She made her way to the women's restroom, and then waited for Rachel to pass through security. Only those on an inmate's approved visitor list could pass through, and even then, the system necessitated a photo ID, a sign-in to a visitor's log, a trip through a metal detector, and photo shoot for a current visitor picture.

Having completed her usual routine, Rachel was to ask the guard if she could use the restroom prior to entering the prison facility. Entering, Rachel ignored Kelsey and continued to the open handicapped stall at the rear of the restroom. Kelsey waited, calmly sweeping until the restroom's only other occupant exited. Then she rushed to the stall with Rachel, turned to lock the door, then hurriedly switched clothes with her friend. Out of her oversized scrubs, she also pulled a long, blonde wig, which she quickly affixed to her head.

She looked up to see Rachel zipping up the cleaning scrubs.

"This will work!" Rachel whispered. "We'll try to buy you as much time with Phillip as possible, but you need to work quickly."

Kelsey nodded, feeling a wave of uncertainty. This was too dangerous and complicated. Maybe she should have just sent Rachel in to try to extract more information from Phillip.

Kelsey stilled her quivering lips and nodded. Rachel had tried before with no results. It was her turn. And with so much at stake, she was open to using tactics Rachel might be hesitant to use. Getting a job done is what Kelsey did, and this time would be no different.

"Snow White is ready," Rachel announced to Dawson and Garrett.

With each member of the team wearing an earpiece, they would hopefully be able to communicate and warn of any threats while enacting the intricate plan.

"Hollywood, is Bond in position?" Rachel asked, stuffing her own hair into a long dark wig the same shade as Kelsey's natural hair.

"Yes, he made it through—"

"Wait a minute," came Garrett's whisper over the earpiece. "What did you just call me? Bond? As in *James Bond?* That's my Rachel-nickname?"

Silence. No one dared answer.

"That's awesome!" he whispered fiercely.

"Great," Kelsey muttered. "Now there will be no living with him."

Dawson chuckled, "Alright, Snow White, back to business. It's your show. The guard to take Rachel to Phillip's cell has just arrived. I arranged for the previous guard to be called off on an errand, so no one will recognize the switch."

Wasting no time, Kelsey walked out the restroom door, leaving Rachel to take her place as the cleaning lady. Dawson was manning the computer side of things, which made Kelsey a little nervous. Dawson was usually a physical, not a technical agent. But since she and Rachel had hacked the system prior to leaving the truck, she thought Dawson should be able to handle things while Garrett, disguised as a prison employee, took the role of lookout and bodyguard for the operation.

With blonde head held high, Kelsey confidently walked to the center guard station. She flashed her best Rachel-smile to one of the guards.

He glanced at the ID in his hand, then back to her. "Rachel Saunders?" he questioned.

Please don't look at the height! Please don't look at the height! "Yes!" she answered quickly.

The guard smiled back at her. "Your ID doesn't do you justice!"

"I don't think driver's license pictures do anyone justice!" Kelsey shot back, her tone relaxed and laughing.

"True," the guard acknowledged. "I'm sure mine could double as a mug shot! Right this way, I'll take you to see your brother."

Standard procedure stipulated that her ID be held until she left, so she wasn't out of the woods yet, but at least she'd made it through the first hurdle.

She followed the guard out the administration side into the actual prison building. Whenever they passed someone, Kelsey tried to unobtrusively keep her face averted on the off-chance that someone who knew the real Rachel would recognize her as an imposter.

"I'm sure you already know this," the guard said, turning over his shoulder to speak as he walked. "But I haven't escorted you previously, so I should probably explain the procedures. Normally, visitors are met by their respective inmates in the visiting room. However, Phillip Saunders is isolated from other inmates, due to concerns for his safety. I will take you directly to his cell. You may speak to him and then let me know when you are finished. Be aware that meetings are monitored visually for safety, and any conversations may be recorded. You may not have any contact with the prisoner other than a brief greeting, such as a hug, at the beginning and end of your visit, if you so choose."

This was all information that Kelsey already knew. Because Phillip himself had been concerned his terrorist ties might make him a target, he had been isolated since arriving at the prison. But in Kelsey's mind, she suspected that Phillip knew more than he pretended, which was the real reason he may be targeted by someone wishing to eliminate the threat.

Kelsey followed the guard through a series of security doors and down halls. Some halls were lined with cells while others were blank walls. She tried to follow their route on her mental map based on the one Rachel had shown her of the prison, but it was difficult with so many turns.

The common thread throughout was the echo of their shoes. It was a hollow, empty sound that only served to make Kelsey feel more nervous and exposed. In an environment where every little sound magnified, it was difficult to imagine that any pretense could be maintained, any secrets concealed.

Entering through one last security door, they finally stopped at a cell. The guard unlocked it and moved aside.

"Mr. Saunders, your sister is here to see you." To Kelsey, he turned and said, "When you're done, just press that button over there in the corner, and I'll come get you."

"Thank you," Kelsey responded, even as her gaze collided directly with that of the convicted murderer and domestic terrorist, Phillip Saunders.

She held steady, like a childhood staring match, almost daring him to rat her out to the guard. Though her heart pounded uncomfortably, she knew she couldn't show hesitation or weakness. To be willing to talk to her, Phillip had to respect her. Kelsey was confident that Phillip wouldn't say anything about her not being his sister. He was too curious for that; she could see it in the light of amusement in his eyes.

The guard turned and relocked the cell, enclosing Kelsey inside with Phillip. Yet they waited, the silence thick with tension, caught in their staring match, until the guard reached the exterior security door.

The instant, the door slammed shut, sending the guard out of earshot, Phillip spoke. "Well, it's nice to see you again, Kelsey. I assume if you went to all the trouble of paying me a visit, then you've also handled the security feed so we can have a more private conversation."

"All set, Snow White," came Dawson's voice in her ear, as if answering Phillip's question himself.

"Yes," Kelsey confirmed to Phillip. "The guards only ever see the visual feed, but not the audio, unless it is specifically accessed for some later reason. We have arranged for any recording of our conversation to be lost in translation, so to speak."

Kelsey had met Phillip once before, at the Saunders' ranch when she had been called in on the investigation that led to Phillip's arrest seven months ago. Other than a brief introduction, Kelsey didn't know that they'd ever spoken, and yet he'd known instantly who she was.

Kelsey studied him, comparing him to the man she had met briefly. The judicial process had passed very quickly for Phillip, especially since he'd accepted a plea bargain. Months in prison did not seem to have taken a large toll on him. He still appeared handsome and fit. His blonde hair and classic, sculpted features reminded her of Rachel, though he was paler than she remembered, and his eyes looked different. Was it possible that imprisonment had mellowed and humbled the prideful, arrogance that had been so much a part of Phillip Saunders?

Kelsey was too realistic to hope for that; she would settle for simply locating a tiny kink in his armor.

"I need information," Kelsey said, forgoing any pleasantries. She didn't know how long she had to speak to Phillip, but the longer it took, the greater the chance that either their ruse would be discovered, or the government agents who pursued them would catch up.

"I'm sorry you wasted your trip," Phillip said, crossing his arms in front of him. "You should already know that both the authorities and Rachel have extracted every bit of information possible from me, repeatedly."

"I need that which was impossible for the others to extract," Kelsey said easily. "I don't need the general mish-mash you fed them. No, what I need is specific, and something I know you have."

She paused, letting the curiosity pique in his eyes. Then she continued. "We know who you were working with. We know why. The problem is that we have no evidence with which to convict the vice president of the United States."

Phillips eyebrows lifted, not in surprise, but in interest, as if she had caught his attention. "That does seem to be a problem," he said, his tone slow and wary. "But I don't know why you think I can help you. If I'd had evidence like that, then I would have relinquished it long ago for a lesser sentence."

"Wrong," Kelsey said flatly.

Phillip blinked in surprise, much to Kelsey's satisfaction. She instinctively knew that the more off-guard she kept him, the greater chance he would do something uncharacteristic. She wasn't willing to be put off by the song and dance he gave everyone else. She knew he had information, and she intended to get it.

"You were headed to jail either way," she explained, pinning him with her gaze. She needed to assess the impact of every word. If she was close to the truth, even a man with a poker face like Phillip might have a tell. "The question was if you would make it to jail alive. And since you are here, I assume you have something on Lewis that she doesn't want to get out. You are too much of a liability for her to let live. And you're too smart to not collect a hefty insurance policy."

Kelsey stepped forward, not releasing Phillip's gaze for even a breath of time.

Phillip's face showed no emotion, yet a tiny muscle in his right cheek twitched with tension.

She had him. "My guess is that you made it known that, upon your death, a large amount of evidence would be immediately transferred to the appropriate authorities. You are not the kind of guy to not have a backup plan. It's very likely that you even have a backup to your backup. And now, I need you to tell me where to locate said backup plan.

Phillip looked away, though the end of the staring match in no way relieved the tension in the small cell. As if weary, he stepped over to the standard, green-clad prison bed and sat down with a sigh. "You're a smart woman, Kelsey. Assuming that your theory has a shred of truth in it, you're stupid to think I would hand over the one thing that's keeping me alive."

"Come on, Kelsey," came Dawson's ragged whisper. "Push him hard. You don't have all day."

Completely ignoring Dawson's intrusion, Kelsey stayed focused on Phillip. "You may think you're keeping yourself alive, but you aren't; you're just buying time. Eventually Lewis will have enough power that any evidence you can produce will be inconsequential. In the likely event that she eventually becomes president, she will be untouchable. She will call your bluff. It may be today or several months or even years from now. But, any way I look at it, you're a dead man."

"That's not going to matter to him, Kelsey!" Dawson snorted. "We're on a timeline here. Bribe him. Threaten him. Just get the info and get out!"

"Back off, Daws!" came Garrett's fierce whisper. "She knows what she's doing. Sit back and shut up. Let her do her job!"

Kelsey longed to rip the earpiece out and step on it. Only later would she indulge in a thrill of pleasure over the fact that Garrett had defended her.

In a deceptively innocent tone, Rachel drove home her final blow. "The real question is not if you can save yourself, you can't—but you may be able to save your family."

"What are you talking about?" Phillip asked, wary and slightly incredulous, as if she was talking to a fish about walking on land.

Kelsey understood his reaction. After all, if nothing else, his actions should make perfectly clear that he didn't care one whit for his family. But Kelsey viewed things from a different angle. No matter what one did, even to the point of killing your abusive father, that in no way meant there was a lack of love and caring.

"Oh, you put on a good show of pretending not to care about your parents or Rachel," Kelsey assured. "But all of them are rather frequent visitors here—your only visitors, right? My guess is that the 'not caring' is your way of protecting them. The instant Ms. Vice President calls your bluff, she'll kill you and your entire family. You've had the most contact with them, and she won't take the risk that they know something."

"I'm still not sure what makes you think that I care," Unable to hide his agitation, Phillip stood and paced the cell. From the bed, to the silver toilet in the corner, and back again. "If you recall, Rachel shot me. That isn't really an endearing gesture for sibling love."

"You could have killed her on multiple occasions and you didn't," Kelsey pointed out, undeterred. "Now, maybe you would have pulled the trigger in the parking garage, but killing her yourself is different than someone else doing it, especially when that someone is the reason you're in prison."

Tiring of standing, Kelsey casually leaned against the wall and watched him pace, by her mere pose conveying that she was in control. "What you don't seem to realize is that the investigation has continued without your cooperation. Rachel is smart. She knows the vice president is the kingpin. Even now, she is in danger, working to find evidence against her. And Lewis is using all of her resources to stop us. This has to end now. Either we stop her or she kills all of us. And your parents will be collateral damage, maybe taken out by a rather convenient car accident."

So Kelsey may have exaggerated slightly about Rachel's initial involvement in the investigation, but she certainly knew who they were up against now, if only by the fact that she was currently listening in with the rest of Kelsey's team!

"My parents know nothing," Phillip bit out, emotion spilling out for the first time.

"But she will assume that they do. She has to! The risk is too great otherwise."

Phillip moaned and his hands came up to hold his head. "I wish she would have just left it alone. I had it under control."

"Have you ever known her to give up on something?" Kelsey ventured. "This technically wasn't even her case, and yet she's determined to finish it."

"She's always been like that, even when we were kids." Phillip sighed heavily and paused for a long moment, thinking. He stood and walked over to the window. It was high on the wall and frosted so as not to see out. Yet he stood there as if he could, watching intently as the meager light fell over him.

"Kelsey," Dawson voice spoke warily in her ear. "I hope you're going somewhere. A trip down memory lane doesn't lead anywhere."

"Let her be, Hollywood," came Rachel's strained voice. "She's getting through to him."

"But the longer we take…"

"The greater the likelihood, I'll have to desert my post to keep you quiet," hissed Garrett.

Finally, Phillip turned and looked directly at Kelsey. He spoke in a sing-song voice, as if lost in memories, yet his eyes were clear and fixed directly on her.

She knew that his tone and his message were two separate things. This was it. He was giving her information.

Chapter 11

"You're right about a lot of things," Phillip said, his tone almost dreamlike. "I have fond memories of when Rachel and I were kids. I've had a lot of time to think about those times. I remember these pictures of camping and playing together. I have a photo album of happy times in my head. Even now, with so much changed, Rachel is really the only one I would ever trust. She always has been, from the very beginning. Do you understand?"

"Yes, I think I do," Kelsey answered, somewhat hesitantly.

She thought she might have heard Dawson snort in derision, but she couldn't be sure.

Phillip obviously still felt it too risky to say things outright, but was telling her where to find the evidence. She just had to unravel the clues.

"I don't know what happened," he mused. "We grew up and changed. Rachel is like my parents. She's a good person. I'm not sure what happened to me."

Kelsey thought. Feelings of this sort were not her specialty. She was much more comfortable stuffing emotions in. Fortunately, she did know someone who was a lot more emotionally healthy than herself. "Rachel would probably give credit to God and say that He is the one that made the difference in her life," she said, relieved she had found something appropriate to say.

Dawson was likely squirming like his feet were on hot pavement. The poor guy was out of his element, manning the computers. It was no wonder he was worried. And now, with the absence of Phillip's body language, it would be impossible to understand that his words were more than idle rambling. Now, eager for more clarification on his clues, Kelsey knew she had to continue the conversation, even if it both drove Dawson crazy and entered the uncomfortable realm of religion.

"That sounds like my sister," Phillip agreed. "Maybe she's right. My parents certainly are Christians. They raised us in church, and yet it never stuck with me. Now it's too late."

"Rachel would say it's never too late." Rachel had better be listening. Kelsey was doing her proud.

"And what would *you* say?" Phillip shot back.

Kelsey blinked, startled. So parroting Rachel wasn't going to be enough after all. She hesitated, and then she spoke slowly, pondering her words even as they escaped her dry lips. "I don't pretend to be a Christian. But I imagine if God was really God, He would be big enough to forgive any amount of wrongdoing at any time."

"So what's your problem?" Phillip persisted. Once again crossing his arms and staring at her unflinching. If that's what you think, why aren't you a Christian?"

Was this going somewhere? She had hoped Phillip would offer more clues or information, but now she was concerned that Dawson was right. Was Phillip just giving her the run-around?

Kelsey licked her lips, deciding that she really didn't have a choice but to play along. "God doesn't like me."

Phillip scoffed. "I can't imagine I'm His favorite person either."

"But you made choices, mistakes that led to the bad things in your life. I'm not saying that I've not made mistakes, but it seems like a God who is supposedly loving, wouldn't have allowed some of the events in my life to happen."

Phillip shrugged and matched her posture by leaning casually against the wall opposite her. "He's God. I guess He's entitled to do what He wants. Maybe the trouble is that you and He aren't on the same page. Not that I'm on His page either, but Rachel always seems to have some hope that if she allows God to work in her life, He has some kind of master plan and can bring good from the bad. "

And now he was the one parroting Rachel?

"And what good can come out of your bad?" Kelsey asked quietly, hoping to, once again, turn the tables on him and direct the conversation back to a more useful avenue.

That telltale muscle in Phillip's cheek twitched right before he answered, his voice quiet and flat. "I don't know that there is any. It's too late for me. The more I think about it, the more I think my parents and Rachel are right in that God is the only one who can help me. I can't fix things, and even if I turn to God, He won't send me back in time to right my wrongs." He paused as, once again, his eyes bore fiercely into Kelsey's. "But if I could, I'd go back to the beginning. I wouldn't let Rachel go on that stupid trip to New York. I'd hide her infernal suitcase that started this whole mess and undo everything from the last year and a half. I'd hand in evidence the first time I was approached and take up ranching like I always should have!"

"Kelsey, we've got a problem," Dawson's voice rasped. "The guard is trying to access the audio."

"Why?" Rachel protested. "There's no cause for that! No safety, no—"

"I don't know, maybe he's bored with it taking so long! But he's going to figure out very shortly that there's a problem."

Kelsey rushed over and hit the call button, hoping it would distract the guard into retrieving her instead of listening to the malfunctioning audio system!

Obviously understanding that their visit was over, Phillip spoke hurriedly, "Kelsey, I need you to understand something. I know what you did for my mom. I didn't send those people to my aunt's house. She's my mom. I would never…"

"I know," Kelsey answered, clearly remembering the incident from seven months ago where she'd had to protect his mom from multiple gunmen.

"You know how this is going to end," Phillip whispered, his voice raspy.

As their eyes locked one last time, Kelsey understood. Even with the clues shrouded and vague, Phillip still believed that, just by communicating with her, he had very likely signed his death certificate.

"Not if I'm fast."

"But if you aren't. I need you to do what you did before."

Kelsey swallowed. If this all went south, he wasn't asking her to save him; he was asking her to save his family.

"I will. I promise."

The guard entered, his face troubled. He wordlessly let Kelsey out of the cell, relocked it, and turned to lead her back through the maze to retrieve her ID.

Kelsey paused, turning back to Phillip Saunders one last time. For all his crimes, all his sins, he was surprisingly *normal*. He wasn't a psychopath like others who carried a similar rap sheet. He was more like a man who had made poor choices and found himself doing things he'd once never dreamed himself capable. And a tiny part of Kelsey's hard heart felt sorry for him.

"Phillip, one thing I've learned from many years of therapy is that regret doesn't achieve anything," she called through the bars separating them.

"What about redemption?" he asked, his voice strained.

The guard opened the door and Kelsey followed. Pausing at the threshold, she spoke one last time, eyes forward, not looking at Phillip, but letting her voice carry in hope to a desperate sinner. "I think that's the only thing that does."

Chapter 12

Something was wrong. The friendly guard from before was now silent, soberly leading the way back through the maze of hallways.

Kelsey scrambled to come up with some casual comment to break the tension, but everything she thought had the potential of making things worse. She really didn't want to give him the opportunity to ask questions!

With each step, an awful certainty grew in Kelsey's mind. Their cover was blown. Kelsey knew it; but there was nothing she could do about it and no way to prevent the coming chain of events.

The guard hadn't quite figured things out. He was suspicious and confused, but it was only a matter of time. Once he went back and checked the audio recording, he would know that something was wrong. At that point, it all would unravel very quickly. The question was if they could get out before he alerted everyone and possibly locked down the facility.

By Kelsey's calculations, they were only about halfway back to the visitors' check-in area when they passed another guard.

"Hey, Neilsen, do you have a sec to take Miss Saunders back to the front? I need to go check something with one of my prisoners."

"Sure," the young guard answered, immediately stepping in to lead the way.

Kelsey longed to say something to delay him, but all she could manage was a polite, "Thank you for your time."

Her former escort nodded and hurried back the other direction.

"I hope there isn't a problem," Kelsey said. Though she directed it at the new guard, she said it more for her team's benefit, to let them know that there *was* a problem. What she really wanted to do was yell for Garrett to take the guard out before he alerted anyone else!

"I'm sure it's fine," the guard named Neilsen assured. "Abbott is a good guard, but he can be overly-cautious."

"I can't get at him without some help!" Garrett's voice hissed through the earpiece. "There are cameras everywhere! Let me know when you've taken care of the witnesses!"

"I can't!" Dawson answered. "I think they discovered something, or their passwords were reset automatically. I'm still logged on, but I can't do anything other than watch the security feeds!"

This was going downhill fast. Their only option was to get out of the way.

Kelsey asked the guard for the time. At his answer, she startled, "Oh, that's later than I thought," she responded worriedly. "Do you think we can hurry? I have an appointment I need to get to!"

"Oh, sure!" the guard said, and happily increasing his pace. He seemed more like a boy scout than a prison guard. In Kelsey's opinion, he was much too young, too freckled, and too chipper to spend his days working with hardened criminals.

"Ummmm, we have a problem." Dawson whispered. "A bunch of FBI vehicles just pulled into the parking lot."

Kelsey, increased her pace until she was almost overtaking her guide.

"Wow, you are in a hurry!" he exclaimed. "You must have a hot date to get to."

"Something like that," Kelsey answered, flashing him a smile.

"The guard is checking the audio recording now," Dawson reported. "No dice. He's upset. Picking up his phone and making a call."

Kelsey held her breath and braced herself, sure that alarms would go off any second. She pushed through the door, entering the administrative section.

Dawson spoke again. "He hung up. Oh no… "

"Dawson what is it?" came Rachel's strained whisper.

"He cut both audio and visual feeds to Phillip's cell. He's going in."

" Garrett get in there!" Rachel agonized.

"I can't! I'm not even close! I'm shadowing Kelsey, just like we planned!"

The voices in Kelsey's ear fell silent, but it was a fear-laden, foreboding silence. They were helpless.

"I'd like my ID back, please," Kelsey said casually. "Rachel Saunders."

The guard at the desk handed her the card. "Have a nice day."

With a quick nod and thanks to her guide, Kelsey hurried toward the glass double doors. Almost there. She longed to break into a sprint, but didn't dare. Instead, her calves hurt as she rushed, threading her way through people, with her eyes on her destination.

She stepped through the doorway, right as an alarm sounded. Giving up on walking, she lightly sprinted forward, right into the chest of a guard stepping out of a station to the right of the entrance.

"Miss Saunders," the guard said stiffly, holding her at arm's length. "I'm glad I caught you. We're going to need you to answer some questions. Am I to understand that you just visited with your brother?"

"Yes.

"Ma'am, we just received a report that, just now, a guard found Phillip Saunders in his cell dead. Apparently you were the last one to see him alive."

A scream of agony ripped through the earpiece. Kelsey stopped breathing, shock rippling with tremors through her body.

Rachel's brother was dead. As long as she lived, she would forever remember the sound of the raw grief in her friend's scream.

Kelsey felt the blood drain from her face, and air still wouldn't fill her lungs. "You have to be mistaken," she whispered hoarsely. "I just saw him. He was perfectly fine when I left."

"Ma'am, we're going to need to ask you some questions. If you will come this way…"

Three men in suits appeared suddenly, surrounding Kelsey and the guard.

"We might need to preempt you on that," one spoke, flashing a cocky grin. "This is Rachel Saunders? We're the FBI. We're going to need to take her into our custody."

"But her brother was just killed!" The guard protested, open-mouthed. "I have my orders to take her to the warden. We need to get her statement."

"We will email it to you. Or would you prefer a text? Right now, she's coming with us."

"I'm sure whatever you need can wait until after she sees the warden," The guard's mouth drew a firm line. "I have my orders; you can sort things out with him."

"And we have ours, which I'm pretty sure outrank yours," the agent's tone dripped condescension. "Are you even sure this is Rachel Saunders? According to our records, Rachel Saunders is currently in Montana with her fiancé. We consider this woman a person of interest in our current federal investigation. Any problem you have in your prison is your problem. If you need assistance or access to any of our prisoners, then those requests need to be made through the proper channels."

The guard looked at Kelsey suspiciously. "I need to speak with my superior about that. This is a federal prison, and I still don't see how your jurisdiction trumps ours." Turning to Kelsey, he said, "Ma'am, you wait right here while I make a call. Should only take a minute."

One of the younger agents groaned and turned to the one who'd been doing the speaking for the group. "Do we seriously have to play nice?"

"I don't."

Kelsey's heart leapt with adrenaline at the sound of Garrett's words, right as he jumped the FBI agent closest to the corner.

Kelsey immediately snapped a roundhouse kick at the agent nearest her. Hitting him in the chest, he stumbled backward, fighting for breath.

The last agent went for his gun. As the gun came level, Kelsey stepped forward, hitting the weapon up with her left hand at the same time she pushed forward hard with her right, grabbing the barrel of the gun and wrenching it with a force she knew would break the agent's index finger. The entire movement happened in a split second, and the gun appeared in Kelsey's hand and leveled at her would-be attacker.

The other agent, stumbled forward again, still disoriented and not seeming to realize Kelsey was now armed.

Keeping her eyes on the agent she'd just disarmed, Kelsey planted a reverse kick in the approaching agent's gut. With a series of grunts, she heard Garrett finally knock him over with a well-aimed punch.

The disarmed agent continued to scream in pain, grabbing at his right hand.

Garrett quickly relieved him of his own handcuffs and joined his injured hand with his other one behind his back.

The other two agents were barely conscious, but still moving, trying to pick themselves up, but they froze as soon as they saw the gun in Kelsey's hands aimed confidently their direction. She held steady while Garrett quickly relieved them of all other weapons and handcuffed them with their own cuffs to match their coworker.

"Wish we had some tranquilizers," Garrett muttered, quickly finishing the job.

But both of them knew they had no time to do anything but leave the agents and hope they could escape with Rachel and Dawson before the vanquished agents roused too much backup.

Casually waving goodbye, Garrett pulled Kelsey with him toward the parking lot. She kept the gun trained on them as long as possible, finally turning to run when the door to the guard shack opened. She knew the scene of three FBI agents unconscious, incapacitated, and handcuffed, with his potential witness nowhere in sight, wasn't the situation the guard was expecting. But Kelsey and Garrett weren't willing to stick around to see what happened next.

They ran to where they had left Dawson's truck under a tree at the back corner of the parking lot. But before they reached the doors, Dawson and Rachel hopped out.

"We have approximately five minutes until the parking lot security cameras come back online," Dawson informed.

Kelsey thought five minutes was a generous estimate. Neither the FBI or the prison security would take five minutes to reach them.

Scanning the faces of her friends only made the panic worse. Nobody knew how to get out. With a wave of nausea, Kelsey realized the worst case scenario was about to happen. Within the next five minutes, they would all very likely be captured or killed. And they had no escape.

Chapter 13

"Making them reboot the system was the best Rachel and I could do," Dawson reported, "but I don't think it's enough. We can't take the truck. They know Rachel arrived in it, so we won't make it past the security checkpoint. With prison guards and the FBI onto us, I'm not sure what our options are."

Kelsey looked from Dawson to Rachel. Rachel's eyes were red and puffy, but she was perfectly in control, though maybe not quite up to plotting their escape. Like a good agent, she had stuffed her emotions deep to do her job. Unfortunately, Kelsey knew too well that all-encompassing grief would return.

"We need another vehicle," Garrett said, turning to peruse the assortment of cars and trucks in the visitor parking lot around them

"We don't have a slim jim," Dawson said thoughtfully. "Do you know any tricks?"

Kelsey interrupted, "I just broke an FBI agent's finger. I'm not sure what the jail time on that offense is, but I'm not really interested in adding 'grand theft auto' to my resume."

Rachel looked at her in understanding. "Poor guy must have pulled a gun."

Kelsey nodded, even as Garrett brushed off her objection.

"I don't think we have a choice," Garrett said. "According to the rap sheet the government already has on you, stealing a car will be the least of your sins."

"I know some vehicles are easier to break into than others," Dawson mused.

Kelsey rolled her eyes as the men began discussing the best ways to steal a car.

The security cameras would come back online at any minute, and they still wouldn't have a way out. Besides, chances were good that with known security system problems, the entire facility would soon be locked down with no vehicles passing out. Except maybe…

Tuning out the men's discussion, Kelsey turned around and walked to the three standard-issue black FBI vehicles parked in the row behind them. Kelsey swallowed. Three vehicles very likely carried more than three agents, so that meant they could be interrupted by those other agents at any time. It wouldn't take long for those they'd already dispatched to call for backup and point them in Kelsey and Garrett's direction.

While the men stayed busy with their discussion, Kelsey went to each black FBI SUV and tried the door handle. When the second one opened, having been left unlocked, she hopped up on the seat and looked at the keyhole.

She felt Rachel's presence without looking.

"Drill?" she asked.

Her friend handed her an electric drill. She looked at Rachel with raised eyebrows, then bent over the keyhole. Rachel was usually well-prepared, but this seemed impressive, even for her.

"The truck had a nice toolbox in back," Rachel simply explained. "Dawson and Garrett got it out, but are still discussing the best technique. I figure we have about one minute. No pressure."

Kelsey focused, carefully drilling the keyhole and removing the lock pins that allowed the car to start. She drilled about the length of a key, then removed the drill, and repeated the drilling. Kelsey knew she should do it once more, just to be sure, but she didn't have the time to spare.

"Screwdriver," she requested, putting her hand out until Rachel plopped the requested item into her palm. She quickly inserted the screwdriver into the keyhole and turned. The engine roared to life. Rachel hopped in the back and Kelsey backed up and pulled up next to Garrett and Dawson.

"Get in!" Kelsey urged the open-mouthed men.

Garrett blinked. "She is *not* driving," he objected.

"Fine. Dawson, you drive."

Kelsey hopped over to the passenger seat while Garrett slid into the back beside Rachel.

"The only way out is to get the security guys to believe we're FBI," Kelsey explained.

As they neared the security checkpoint, she thought better of her position, and dove into the backseat as well. Their only chance was to bluff their way out, and their bluff would fall to pieces if she was recognized or matched a description.

Rachel, probably thinking the same thing, joined Kelsey on the floor of the vehicle, trying to stay hidden. Then Garrett stretched out on the seat above them, working to keep himself out of sight. Though the windows of the SUV were tinted dark, it would be better if Dawson appeared to be alone.

Right before she ducked her head, she saw Dawson slide his sunglasses over his eyes and roll down his window.

"I'm sorry, sir," a guard at the security station said. "We are on lockdown. No one goes in or out."

"I don't think that applies to the FBI," Dawson said calmly. "We have a situation that needs attention ASAP."

"I have orders, but they didn't really say anything about the FBI."

"Check my plates, as well as your own records," Dawson said. "My fellow agents and I arrived not long ago. Three vehicles total. The warden was to be notified immediately. Now a situation has occurred in the prison, and it is vital that I get out to update my superiors in person."

Kelsey heard the shuffling of papers.

"Hurry," Dawson barked. "I really don't have all day."

"Ummm… I see the records, but I should probably verify things through the warden first."

"He already sent verification—me! I'm an FBI agent, for Pete's sake. If you don't let me out of here right now, I'm going to make sure you get janitor duty here for the next four years!"

"Ummm… maybe I could. Sir, do you have like a badge or something?"

"I have a government issued license plate! Check it!" Nevertheless, Kelsey heard Dawson's weight shift on the seat. "Here's my badge. Now let me out of here!"

The security gate opened and Dawson drove out, turning and tearing down the highway, as if on a mission, or maybe just escaping a federal prison.

"Dawson, what did you show him?" Rachel asked, climbing up to the front passenger seat.

"I showed him my badge, just like he wanted. He just needed to see something; I don't think it mattered what. I probably could have shown him my library card and gotten away with it. As it was, I flashed him my Homeland Security badge for a half second, which apparently was good enough."

Dawson was awesome! He had handled that entire situation masterfully, and Kelsey knew his skill was the only reason they had made it out of the prison.

Garrett slid back into his seat and immediately took out the iPad Andrews had sent. Without a word, he ducked his head and busied his fingers.

Kelsey's annoyance immediately flared.

Dawson suddenly let out an exasperated breath. "So where am I going now?" he asked. "We went through all of that for nothing! Kelsey didn't manage to get anything out of Phillip, and now he's dead. Such waste! What are we going to do now?"

And just like that, Dawson's awesomeness went out the window.

"What do you mean, I didn't get anything out of him?" Kelsey shot back. "I thought I was supposed to get evidence against the vice president!"

"Yes! And yet you came away with nothing!"

"Were you not listening?" Kelsey gritted out. "He told me where he hid the evidence. Now we just need to retrieve it."

Dawson paused, as if second guessing himself. "No, he didn't. He rambled on about his childhood and feeling guilty."

"Exactly," Kelsey said with conviction. "He gave me everything I needed to know. I just have to unravel the clues."

"Ok, so where is it?" Dawson questioned, impatience and doubt dripping from his tone. "Where are we headed?

Kelsey shut her eyes, feeling the pressure. Dawson was aggravating her, but she could understand his stress. All of their lives were on the line. Everything depended on her figuring Phillip's clues out. Fortunately, she had an exceptional memory and could remember, almost verbatim, their entire conversation.

Her mind focused on what he'd said at that exact moment when his eyes and his tone were sending two separate messages. "I have a photo album of happy times in my head.... Rachel is really the only one I would ever trust. She always has been."

Kelsey's eyes flipped open. "Rachel, do you have a photo album of when you and Phillip were kids?"

"Sure. My mom has a ton of them."

"No, do *you* have any?"

Rachel paused. "I have a kind of scrapbook I made when I was a kid. My mom would always order double prints and give me the extras. I'd cut them up and glue them in a book. It's not really much of a photo album though. I've never really been artistic, even as a child."

"Where is your scrapbook?"

"At our apartment in New York. When I moved to New York after joining Homeland Security, I found where my mom had stuck it in a box for me."

"That was before Phillip's arrest," Kelsey said. "Maybe it wasn't your mom who put it in that box."

Rachel looked at Dawson. "It looks like we're going to New York."

"That's easier said than done. We're in a stolen FBI vehicle and have the entire U.S.

government on our tail. Anyone have an idea on how to get to New York alive?"

"Turn left," Garrett said suddenly.

"Where?" Dawson demanded.

"There!"

Swerving, Dawson turned onto a country road that didn't seem to boast much travel, or even a street name.

The road curved sharply around a copse of trees, and then opened up into a clearing where a helicopter stood at attention.

"There's our ride to New York," Garrett announced.

"How did you manage that?" Kelsey asked. "Another one of your blackmailing 'friends?'"

"No," Garrett said with a withering look Kelsey's direction. "As soon as we were clear of the prison, I contacted Andrews through the secure connection he had provided in the tablet. When I told him we had a location on the evidence, he immediately set up an extraction."

"Wait a minute," Dawson said, pulling to a stop. "That was before Kelsey said she had the location. Was I the only idiot who missed that she got that information from Phillip?"

"I'd think that, by now, you'd be used to being the only idiot," Garrett ribbed. "By the way

Kelsey handled the conversation, I figured she'd gotten what she needed. After all, she hadn't resorted to the more creative interrogation methods. Besides, Kelsey gets the job done. I knew she wouldn't leave empty handed."

Kelsey said nothing, though she was surprised. That was high praise coming from Garrett. His confidence in her somehow made her feel differently toward him. Maybe not so antagonistic. They had always been like oil and water, seeming to work against each other more than together. But maybe Garrett respected her more than it seemed.

The men hopped out of the SUV, and Rachel and Kelsey followed.

Heading for the helicopter, Dawson slapped Garrett on the back, saying, "I'm sorry, Mr. Bond. I guess I kind of stole your thunder. After all, you're usually the idiot where Kelsey is concerned!"

"Umm… guys?" Kelsey said, trying to get their attention while keeping her hand on her gun. She looked at the helicopter suspiciously.

The pilot hopped out, and she drew her gun. At the action, the men's attention snapped from their ribbing to her weapon.

The pilot immediately put his hands up, as if in surrender.

"How do we know Andrews sent the copter?" she said nervously. "Think about who we are dealing with. How do we know that tablet wasn't a tool in a trap?"

"Are you Kelsey Johnson?" The pilot asked, raising his voice while keeping his hands up.

Kelsey paused, then nodded once.

"Mr. Andrews said that if you or anyone else had reservations to give you a date and time. Does January 23 at 11:53 mean anything to you? Andrews seemed to think that it would."

Kelsey immediately lowered her gun. "It's Andrews," she said stiffly.

Her peers looked at her curiously, but didn't ask, simply taking her word for it and climbing into the copter.

Kelsey took several deep breaths, then climbed in last. Though she appreciated Andrews providing proof of his involvement, that was a hard way to hear it. Andrews had sealed her file himself. He was the only one who knew the significance of that exact moment. It was a moment forever etched in her memory, and her nightmares. It was the moment she pulled the trigger—the same moment listed as her father's official time of death.

And yet, as bad as it hurt, there was something appropriate about a mention of that moment. On that night, she had stopped someone from hurting others. And now, she was on her way to New York to do the same thing.

Chapter 14

"This is the only one you have?" Kelsey asked as Rachel handed her a ragged scrapbook.

"Yes," Rachel confirmed. "My mom has all of the other family photo albums. I really can't imagine that Phillip put anything in that scrapbook."

It definitely looked as if it had been constructed, and loved, by a child. Big colorful writing labeled awkwardly trimmed photos. Kelsey leafed through the bulky, worn pages, finding nothing that could resemble evidence, other than some rather embarrassing photos neither Rachel or Phillip would have liked posted to social media.

"There's nothing else?" Kelsey asked again, feeling despair clouding the horizon.

"No," Rachel said, bending over to search through a box at the bottom of her closet. "All of the other things from my childhood are in Montana. Do you think he could have hidden the evidence there?"

"No, I don't think so," Kelsey said, though now she was beginning to doubt everything. "The way he talked, he would have wanted it near you. He trusted you, and yet you couldn't do anything about something in Montana."

Kelsey flipped through the scrapbook, and then began searching under furniture, in drawers, anywhere she could think of. But since she didn't know what exactly she was looking for, it seemed a lost cause.

Rachel disappeared, only to return about thirty seconds later with a yellow dress draped over her arm. At the sight of the dress, Kelsey knew her friend had raided her closet.

"We're running out of time," Rachel explained. "You need to try on the dress."

Kelsey shot a concerned look at Rachel's tear-stained face. Her brother had just died and men with guns were coming after them, yet she was worried about a bridesmaid dress?

Rachel met her eyes and shrugged, her lips trembling. "Kelsey, it's the only thing keeping me sane right now. I can't think about anything more significant than wedding details, or I'll lose what little control I have."

Kelsey nodded and smiled gently. "I'll be sure to try on the dress in between gathering evidence and staying alive. And if we run out of the mundane, I can even help you make a seating chart for the reception."

Kelsey's phone rang. It was a call from Garrett's pre-arranged burner number.

Garrett spoke quickly. "Time's up. We have company."

"How did they find us so quickly?" Kelsey asked, shocked.

"Don't know. Doesn't matter. You need to get out now."

Kelsey ended the call and grabbed Rachel's scrapbook off the floor. She squished the awkward pages closed, careful that none of the loosely glued papers fell out.

Both Rachel and Kelsey turned and ran for the front door. With Kelsey's hand on the doorknob, her phone rang again.

"You have no exit!" Garrett rushed. "They're moving fast. Front and rear exits are blocked, and they're moving up your way. There's no escape out the front door. It's too late. You'll have to use the backup plan!"

"I don't want to use the backup plan!" Kelsey fumed. "I don't like it!"

"Kelsey Johnson, follow the backup plan right now! You don't have a choice!"

Kelsey hung up the phone and reluctantly followed Rachel to the window.

"Come on, Kelsey," Rachel encouraged, her steady hands offering her friend a hook attached to a cable.

This was a bad idea. Kelsey had never liked this plan, and had made her feelings clear when Garrett and Dawson had first concocted the scheme. The overall plan was for the men to stay on the roof of the apartment building with the helicopter, acting as lookouts, while Kelsey and Rachel went down to the apartment to search for the scrapbook. The thought was that the women would be able to move more swiftly while the men would be ready in case things went south and visitors arrived.

And that's where they were now. With all exits blocked, the men had used equipment found in the helicopter to rig an insane "backup plan." And now Kelsey was expected to follow it and hope that the men kept up their ends.

That was the most difficult part for her— trusting someone enough to know that if she jumped, he would catch her.

Rachel attached her own hook to the belt around her waist and clutched the yellow dress in her arms. "Ready?" she asked.

"No!" Kelsey said, working to get her hook attached. "It won't attach!"

No matter what she tried, the metal clasp would not open to clip to the matching brace at her waist.

Needing both her hands to work the clasp, Kelsey did the only thing she could think of. She opened the neck of her shirt and stuffed the bulky scrapbook inside.

"You don't like this plan either, Rachel," Kelsey accused. "Don't pretend you're any more comfortable with Dawson and Garrett's scheme than I am!"

"No, I don't like it," she said. "But I also know that you trained me that, in this line of work, even if you don't want to, sometimes you have to pull the trigger, or in this case…

The door to their apartment burst open.

Rachel shrieked. "Jump!"

Giving up on the clip, Kelsey gripped the cable in her hands and ran alongside Rachel out the sliding balcony door. They leapt onto the railing, and without hesitation, jumped.

Kelsey had two full seconds of free fall before the cable grew tight in her hands. The yank of her weight on her hands hit like a bungee cord. She grunted, trying to maintain a good hold as she bounced up and settled back down heavily, her weight dangling below.

She immediately felt the tug on her hands, the cable being steadily pulled upward, but she couldn't even look to make sure how Rachel was faring. Her entire attention focused on her hands gripping that cable and supporting her entire weight as she swung to and fro.

Kelsey closed her eyes tightly, not because she was scared of heights, but because she wanted to focus without the dizzying sights swinging as she was drawn upward. She breathed steadily, with hands locked firmly on the cable above her head.

She wasn't too concerned that she would lose her grip. Though she felt the strain, she was in good shape. Multiple reps of pull-ups had made her confident that she could support her own weight for the thirty seconds it would take for the men to get her to the roof.

But she hadn't counted on her sweaty palms. The longer it took, the more moisture slicked the cable. With a strong heave of the cable, her hands slid down a centimeter.

Her eyes flew open. She exhaled slowly, trying not to panic. With a mighty heave, she pulled herself up, repositioning her hands so that the bottom one was now at the top. She hoped to gain a better hold, but the movement added momentum to the sweat-slicked cable. She slid down again. Her heart leapt into her throat, urging her to scream as the cable slipped through her hands. Refusing to give in, she refused to let a sound escape, but gritted her teeth and grabbed hard, the line burning into her hands until she stopped her slide after about eight inches.

A shot rang out, causing Kelsey's already stampeding heart to painfully lurch. She looked down. Men stood on the balcony of her apartment, with weapons raised their direction.

"Hurry!" she heard Rachel shriek.

Kelsey hated feeling helpless. She couldn't just hang there waiting for them to shoot her. Trying not to think about what she was doing, Kelsey began to swing. She moved erratically, making herself the most difficult target possible.

The cable bit into her hands, but she clutched it even harder.

Kelsey thought she might be sick from the combination of motion and adrenaline. The efforts at movement were rapidly tiring her muscles, and she wasn't sure how much longer she could hold on. The ride up had taken what seemed to be much longer than she had ever imagined.

More shots echoed out.

Despite her vice-like grip on the cable, her wet hands began to slip again. She dared not try to readjust her hand position like she had last time. So she waited, knowing she had very little time as the cable slowly slipped.

Just when the cable was slipping more rapidly through her burning fingers, strong hands grasped her forearms, pulling her up over the ledge and onto the roof.

Without a moment to even breathe, Garrett lifted her to her feet and half dragged her to the helicopter whose rotors were already rapidly spinning. He pushed her up into the cockpit ahead of him and climbed up behind her.

Rachel and Dawson were already getting settled in their seats. As soon as Garrett slammed the door, the helicopter lifted into the air.

With shaking hands, Kelsey, put the headphones on that Garrett handed her.

"Are you okay?" He asked through the communicator in his matching headphones.

Not trusting her voice, Kelsey nodded and tried to subtly hide her shaking hands.

But Garrett lifted one of her hands in his and turned it over, revealing angry, red blisters.

"Dawson, I need the first aid kit," Garrett announced, obvious concern lining his voice.

Dawson, wearing has headphones like everyone else, handed him the hard case. "Is she okay?" he asked.

"Her hands are torn up pretty bad," Garrett answered, hurrying to find some bandages and ointment in the kit.

"They should be," Dawson said. "With the way she had to hold herself up… there aren't many people on the planet who could have done that, especially while being shot at. Was your gear not working?"

"No," Kelsey answered, now thankful to distract herself from Garrett's gentle care of her hands. "I couldn't get the clip to release. My only option was to hold the cable myself."

The pilot suddenly uttered a colorful exclamation. "I knew that one of those clips was broken, and I meant to get it fixed. I completely forgot about it until now!"

Garrett startled. By the tension in his hand holding hers, she knew he was furious.

However, for some reason, Kelsey wasn't angry at all. It was done. She had survived, and there was nothing to change what had happened. Instead, a sudden, ridiculous burst of laughter begged to be let out, but out of the corner of her eye, she caught a glimpse of Rachel's face. At the sight of silent tears streaming down her friend's cheeks as she clutched the yellow dress in her lap, the urge fled.

"Rachel, what's wrong?" Kelsey's concern bordered on panic. She had been so busy trying to save herself, she hadn't paid attention to her friend's trip to the roof. Had things not gone well for Rachel either?

Rachel hiccupped and waved her hand. "I'm fine. It was just really hard to watch you struggle and not be able to help, especially after everything with Phillip..." Rachel stopped, struggling to not lose control entirely. Finally, she managed a deep, shaky breath and continued, "I was fine and made it up to the roof a lot faster than you. Garrett and Dawson had to work to not do anything that could cause you to lose your hold."

"I'm fine," Kelsey assured, though she knew the uncontrollable shaking after-effects of adrenaline gave evidence to the contrary.

Garrett continued working on her hands, though she wasn't convinced they needed such ardent attention. She really didn't even feel much pain, though she guessed that could also be attributed to shock.

Garrett's early anger had gradually subsided. After tenderly spreading a salve over the wounds on both hands, he now worked at carefully wrapping each in long, white bandages in such a way that would make a mummy proud.

Kelsey breathed deeply, trying to quiet what felt like vibrations surging through her body, and she wasn't convinced they were completely caused by the helicopter ride. "What's the plan?" she asked, eager to get the focus off her. Being uncomfortably aware of Garrett's gentle, almost reverent care of her injuries, any further distraction would be an added bonus.

As if also anxious for a change of subject, the pilot eagerly replied, "I have my orders to drop Agent Saunders and Agent Tate off at the airport and then take you and Agent Matthews to a safe house. Andrews indicated he would make arrangements to retrieve the evidence from you there, but didn't feel it would be safe to do so in New York."

"I guess our quick trip to Montana is almost over," Dawson said, looking over his shoulder from the front seat to grin at Rachel.

Garrett spoke, filling in the details. "Andrews contacted me while you were in the apartment. He indicated that he's being watched. He doesn't think his messages have been compromised, but he does think they are being traced. That could explain how they found us so quickly. If they know Andrews is helping us, they might suspect we would try to make it back to him in New York. Andrews also said they sent a large contingent to the Homeland Security office. I guess they didn't know where in New York we'd show up, they were just covering their bases."

"Well, it's awfully hard to fly into New York undetected these days," the helicopter pilot said. "If they had even a few details, it wouldn't have been hard to locate us."

"True," Garrett agreed, though he still shot a look of dislike the pilot's direction before turning back to Kelsey. "When I assured Andrews that we had the evidence, he gave orders for an extraction and a safe house."

"Wait a minute," Kelsey said. "You told him we have the evidence?"

"Yes, of course."

"But we *don't* have it!" Rachel said in alarm. "It wasn't in the scrapbook like we thought. We left with nothing. Everything happened so quickly. Then Kelsey couldn't get the cable to clip to her brace and the agents burst through the door. We had to just jump. It wasn't like Kelsey could carry anything, and I didn't know what to take. We'd already looked through the scrapbook."

"You don't have *anything*?" Dawson asked. "All of that was for nothing?"

After finishing the bandaging, Garrett had kept Kelsey's left hand held gently in his. Though strangely reluctant to leave the warm comfort, she took her hand back out of necessity. "I didn't quite leave with nothing," Kelsey said, opening the top of her shirt and cringing in pain as she removed the scrapbook.

Rachel laughed. "But that still doesn't mean we have the evidence."

Kelsey didn't answer, but instead, began flipping slowly through the scrapbook while everyone else attempted to brainstorm what they should do without the evidence. But Kelsey knew it was a rather pointless discussion. Without evidence, there was nothing they could do!

As she idly fingered one of the thick pages in her hand, she suddenly got an idea. The information had to be in this photo album; she was sure of it. There just wasn't another option. But Phillip wouldn't have made the information obvious to anyone flipping through.

Kelsey carefully examined the pages, noting that they were thick and somewhat disfigured from the amount of glue a child had used to put it together. What if the bulkiness wasn't caused by the advanced age of the materials and the inexperienced age of the original artist? Without asking Rachel's permission, she quickly ripped out a page. She then used her pocketknife to slip the blade in between the double thick album paper. Like a seal being broken, a narrow, hollow shell now appeared in between the pages.

She reached inside and took out sheets of papers. Quickly scanning their contents, she saw they were documents, copies of emails, and even bank records. Most importantly, she saw a name clearly listed: Victoria Lewis.

Excitedly, she slid her knife along the edge of the other pages, realizing that each page contained documents, neatly arranged by date.

"I found it," Kelsey said breathlessly. "We have the evidence."

Chapter 15

Kelsey was so tired, she wished she hadn't noticed the surroundings. But with years of training, she could not turn off her senses that performed automatic surveillance no matter her mood or the setting.

She tried to tell herself they were safe. Andrews wouldn't have sent them to somewhere that wasn't completely secure, especially considering the evidence they now held. Everything thus far had gone completely according to plan. The helicopter dropped off Rachel and Dawson without incident, and then flew Garrett and Kelsey to a safe house somewhere near the Hamptons.

But despite her own internal pep talk, her senses were still on high alert. She didn't want to note the luxurious furnishings of the large house. She didn't want to notice the way the subtle lighting reflected off the dark wood trim; didn't want to see the romantic stone fireplace where Garrett was busy lighting a fire to ward off the chill of the empty house.

And she most definitely did not want her mind's analysis: though their previous "safe house" had been the opposite of a romantic getaway, this place could be a movie set for an epic love affair.

What she *wanted* was to find what was sure to be a comfortable bed with lots of pillows and slip into the oblivion of sleep, forgetting that yesterday and today had ever happened, at least until Andrews showed up to collect the evidence that would mark this mission complete.

"We'll need to take shifts," Garrett announced, adjusting the logs so the flames caught.

Kelsey knew keeping watch tonight was necessary. There was too much at stake, no matter how safe they thought they were. But she couldn't help but long for those fluffy pillows.

"I'll take the first shift," Garrett volunteered. "You take some more pain medicine for your hands and get some rest. I'll wake you when it's your turn."

"That isn't necessary," Kelsey objected, unwilling to let Garrett be gallant. "I can take the first shift."

Garrett closed his eyes in frustration. "Johnson, please. Can we not argue over every little thing, just this once? Neither one of us slept last night. We are both exhausted. If you want, tomorrow I'll argue with you over the color of the sky, but for now, find a pillow and a blanket and find out how comfortable the couch is."

"Aren't there bedrooms upstairs?" Kelsey asked. If she was going to sleep first, then maybe there was still a chance that she could escape to an actual bed.

"I'm sure there are, but we need to stay together. The risk is too great for us not to be diligent. I can't protect you if you're upstairs and I'm down here."

Kelsey bit her tongue, really wanting to snap back that she didn't need his protection. She was more than able to take care of herself. But he was right. In the event that something bad happened, they needed to stay together. Though she didn't like to admit it, she would very likely need his protection once her eyes closed. She couldn't guarantee her normal reflexes would be working when in a deep, exhausted sleep.

Garrett looked up at her, as if impatient that she still hadn't moved to follow his instructions. "Now if you really need to sleep in a bed, I'm sure I can go find a bedroom to accommodate both of us." Garrett raised his eyebrows, daring her to react to his flippant remark.

"I'll take the couch," Kelsey flung back, turning immediately to locate a linen closet.

Kelsey soon had a pillow and blanket laid out on the couch facing the fireplace. She nervously lay down, fully clothed, watching Garrett as he sat silhouetted against the flames.

She didn't like the idea of him watching her while she slept. Kelsey was not a good sleeper, but Rachel was the only one who understood that. Since Rachel was Kelsey's roommate, full disclosure of Kelsey's sleeping habits had come through experience.

Maybe it wouldn't happen again. Maybe she'd sleep well tonight. After all, it would only be for a few hours. She didn't have nightmares every night. Hopefully last night had gotten the memories out of her system for a while. Following her rationale, Kelsey was able to push aside any thought of warning Garrett that she may be rather restless. It wasn't his business anyway. Chances were good that she would sleep hard until awakened for her security shift.

"Good night," Garrett said, standing to take a peek through the curtains.

Kelsey didn't bother to respond. Instead, she kept her eyes open, watching as he came back and sat on a chair facing the fireplace. She kept her eyes open as long as possible, seeing Garrett's figure against the dancing flames. Eventually, the hypnotic sight drew her eyes shut involuntarily, and she never remembered the exact moment sleep overtook her.

Instead, the flames of the fire gradually shifted from reality to dream. They grew and somehow surrounded her. She looked around, trying to find an escape, but there was none. Through the orange flames and smoke, she caught sight of a shadow.

"Help!" she screamed.

The figure turned, and she saw her dad's face. Suddenly, a gun was in her hands. She didn't want to pull the trigger. She flexed her finger away from the trigger, trying to drop the gun, but it stayed in her hand as if glued.

Her dad's eyes plead; his lips mouthed the word, *"Please!"*

But, through no will of her own, she felt her finger pull the trigger.

Time slowed. Kelsey saw the bullet leave her gun and travel through the flames. Smoke covered her father's face, and when it cleared, someone else stood in his place.

It was Garrett.

Kelsey screamed.

She heard her own blood-curdling scream echo over and over as the bullet tore into Garrett's chest. She saw the shock on his face and watched the life drain from his eyes as his body began to fall backward.

And still she screamed. She tried to run to him, but something was holding her back.

"Kelsey! Kelsey, it's okay! Wake up, sweetheart. Come on! It's just a dream!"

The words finally broke through as strong arms wrapped around her, pulling her close. With great, shuddering breaths, Kelsey gradually awoke in Garrett's arms.

Sobbing, she clung to him, burying her face in his strong chest and gripping the front of his shirt tightly, as if afraid he would disappear if she let go.

"Shhh," Garrett soothed, repeating words of comfort over and over as he held her close and stroked her hair. "I've got you," he whispered. "Everything is fine. It was just a dream."

It was a full ten minutes before Kelsey's body stopped shuddering and she came to her senses enough to feel embarrassed. "I'm sorry," she hiccupped, drawing away from the shelter of Garrett's arms. "I guess I should have warned you that I sometimes have nightmares. I just didn't think it would happen tonight. I'm fine now, though. So you might as well get some sleep while I keep watch. I doubt I will be risking more sleep tonight!" Kelsey attempted a laugh, but it came out more as a hiccup.

She started to rise off the couch to give Garrett room to stretch out, but Garrett pulled her back down.

"Nightmares about your dad?" he questioned gently.

Kelsey froze. "You know?" she asked hesitantly.

Garrett nodded solemnly, his eyes wary as if he was afraid he might upset her. "Andrews sent me your unedited file on the iPad Dawson delivered. He seemed to think it was important for me to have the full story since our lives were depending on each other. I'm sorry. I would have preferred to wait until you opened up and told me about your past yourself but—"

"I should have told you," Kelsey admitted. "Andrews is right. It was wrong for me not to tell you, especially when it could obviously put your life at risk."

"You mean because you were never cleared to be a field agent?"

Kelsey grimaced. "I assume you read my psych report. I wasn't just never cleared. The psychologist deemed I would be a danger to myself and any agent I worked with if I was allowed to do field work. Andrews should have let me go right there."

"But he didn't. He let you become an expert at the behind-the-scenes work, and he still trusted you enough to send you on some field missions, even without the clearance."

Kelsey sighed, rubbing her temples. "Yes, but those were very specific missions involving someone I was assigned to protect. I'm perfect for those."

"What do you mean?" Garrett asked gently. "I saw the official reports, but Andrews' notes or reasoning wasn't included."

"In a combat situation, I crumble if facing a direct, personal challenge. In short, my psychological makeup won't allow me to protect myself. However, I'm vicious if I'm protecting someone else."

Garrett nodded. "That makes sense. I remember when you were assigned to protect Rachel's mom. The report was that you took out multiple armed assailants. At the time, I remember being mystified as to why you weren't a full-time field agent."

Kelsey shrugged helplessly, still unable to meet Garrett's eyes. "Obviously, the psychologist thought it related to the traumatic experience of killing my father. And massive amounts of therapy hasn't made a difference. I still have the dreams—frequently."

"I read every report and newspaper article I could find on that." Garrett's voice was quiet, though firm with conviction. "Kelsey, you were protecting your mother. It wasn't your fault. You were the only reason she lived that night. Wasn't she in intensive care for a few weeks afterward?"

Kelsey nodded. "Yes, there was never a question of me being brought up on charges. The police even called me a hero." Kelsey made a face. "My mother is still alive, though she's had health problems since then. She has a nice apartment outside the city. Since I'm the only child, I try to see her frequently and make sure she's taking care of herself, though I wouldn't call her completely recovered either. She's had to deal with PTSD in addition to everything else."

"I couldn't find any articles or information about you or your mother following that initial report. I wondered how things turned out."

Kelsey watched the flickering fire, the painful memories dancing in her mind like the flames. "Our story wasn't widely known, thank goodness, so there were no follow-up reports. Of course, my name was kept out of the media since I was a minor. But Andrews knew my history when he hired me. He's always been very supportive and sealed my file and all reports. But a great cover up still doesn't mask all the effects."

Garrett gently took Kelsey's hand. "I don't imagine that it does. I'm sorry that happened to you. No one should have to go through that."

Kelsey appreciated Garrett's care. She knew her past was shocking and a lot to deal with. Part of her was very embarrassed that after all these years, it still affected her so deeply. "I thought that with enough time and therapy things would get better, but they haven't," Kelsey admitted. "Knowing the truth in your head is one thing. Making your psychosis accept that you looked at your father and pulled the trigger when you were sixteen years old is quite another thing."

Kelsey finally looked at him, begging him to understand who she was with all her faults. However, she also realized that if he fully understood, he should head the other direction as fast as he could. "I'm messed up, Garrett. And I likely will never be fixed. If a gun is pointed at my head, I break out in a sweat and drop my weapon. Every time. If I'm protecting someone else, I take out the guy in less than two seconds and pull the trigger without hesitation."

Garrett looked at her steadily. "Then we'll just have to make sure you're always the one protecting me."

A smile broke through, tears once again squeezing out of Kelsey's eyes. "That may be best!" she hiccupped. Was it possible that he could accept her the way she was, faults and all?

Garrett reached out and wiped her tears away with the soft pressure of his fingertips.

"The psychologist assures me that I'm really remarkably well-adjusted for having such trauma," Kelsey said with an attempt at a laugh. "Other than having no personal protective instinct, I really don't have many ill effects."

"Except for the nightmares." Garrett's deep voice somehow seemed comforting in what would otherwise be a painful observation.

Kelsey nodded. "Yes, the nightmares never go away. Rachel has become used to them now and makes nightly trips into my room, if necessary, to wake me up and stop the screaming. Sometimes they are better, and I'll go a month or so without one. They are worse if I'm overly-tired or stressed."

"You dream about your father."

It wasn't really a question, but Kelsey treated it as such. "Yes. Usually it's the same thing, reliving pulling the trigger and seeing my father die."

"Usually, but not always?"

"There can be slight variations. Tonight's dream was different." Kelsey shifted uncomfortably, and she knew she hadn't successfully masked the troubled look on her face. She'd become used to the dreams, so they didn't usually affect her day. But she knew this one would bother her.

"How was it different?" Garrett asked.

Kelsey was silent. He didn't really need to know. It wasn't his business. And yet it felt good to talk to someone. Rachel had been so busy with wedding preparations that they hadn't had a chance for their normal deep conversations lately. And Rachel was the only one Kelsey had ever let close enough to know her in all her brokenness.

Now, Garrett was looking at her so tenderly, as if he really cared and wanted to help make things better. She remembered the comfort of his arms, a comfort she didn't know that she'd ever felt before. If talking to him brought even a fraction of that same comfort…

She spoke softly, not even sure if Garrett would be able to hear. "The gun was in my hand, and I was aiming at Dad, just like usual, but there were flames. I didn't want to pull the trigger, but it happened anyway. Then I saw the bullet leave my gun, headed directly toward him. But his face changed, and my dad wasn't the one standing there. You were. The bullet I shot hit you, and I watched you die."

Garrett wordlessly enfolded her back in his arms. She heard him praying for God to comfort her, which only increased the flow of tears wetting his shoulder.

She felt a gentle kiss to her hair, and Garrett spoke, "Kelsey, I wish I could take the pain away and replace all the memories with good ones. But I think it's actually a good thing that I can't. I like the person you are today, and I wouldn't want to change a single thing about you. That horrible experience, and the memories you still struggle with, have made you into the strong, determined, intelligent woman who stayed with me to do the right thing, even though it risked her life. You are amazing. And if that experience helped contribute to you, then my prayer can only be that God will heal the hurt and use you to do things equal to the amazing person you are. God doesn't waste pain, and I know yours will have a purpose, even as I believe it already has."

Kelsey wanted to admit that she and God weren't exactly on speaking terms, but she didn't. There was something both painful and exciting about Garrett's words, and at the moment, she didn't feel equipped to handle either.

What if he was right? What if God allowed her past for her eventual good? She had spent so much time believing that a loving God couldn't allow something like that. But allowing it didn't mean He liked it. But if He could somehow redeem it... If her life wasn't destined to always be shadowed by her past, maybe she could have hope.

"I thought you didn't like me," she sniffled instead, pushing her other thoughts aside.

Garrett laughed and pulled her away from his shoulder so he could look in her eyes. "You aggravate me like no other woman ever has," he said with a grin. "But *liking* you has never been the problem."

Kelsey nodded as if she understood, but she didn't. "I'm sorry about unloading all of this on you," she said, suddenly feeling awkward and turning to study the fire with great interest. "I know I can be difficult. I'm not exactly a user-friendly partner."

Garrett reached out and turned her chin back toward him, forcing her to look at him again. "Don't apologize. You're you. I like the full package, baggage and all." As if pronouncing a blessing, he placed a gentle kiss on her forehead, then held still, capturing Kelsey's eyes with his own.

Kelsey watched the flames of the slowly dying fire in the reflection of his eyes. Her breath caught at the deep compassion she read in their depths. Completely mesmerized, she watched as they subtly changed and grew darker, almost smoky. She couldn't identify it, but for some reason, her heart began to beat faster and goosebumps prickled over her body, though the room felt warm.

As if drawn together, Garrett came closer. She felt his strong arms at her back gently pulling her near. Her tingling lips parted slightly and she closed her eyes.

Garrett's lips found hers. Kelsey couldn't breathe. It was the most beautiful, intoxicating sensation she had ever experienced, and she never wanted it to end. Quickly, the kiss turned from gentle exploration to hint of something more deep and passionate. Garrett's mouth moved across hers hungrily, and she responded with just as much ardor.

Garrett suddenly ripped his mouth away and stood. He walked to the fireplace, raking his fingers through his hair. Leaning against the mantle, he breathed deeply.

Kelsey worked to catch her breath as well, though her eyes never left Garrett as he obviously worked to put distance between them.

After several minutes, he finally turned back, an amused smile on his lips. "I was afraid of that."

"Of what?" Kelsey, asked, her voice still breathless.

"I've always been afraid I'd never survive kissing you."

Kelsey threw a pillow, hitting him directly in his laughing face.

But somehow, she knew he was right. Her world would never be the same after kissing Garrett Matthews.

Chapter 16

Time to wake up, sleepyhead," Kelsey said, nudging Garrett with her foot.

She still didn't understand why he'd chosen to sleep on the floor rather than the couch, but she had to admit it was rather convenient for attempting to awaken the bear.

She nudged again with her foot, this time, a little harder.

Garrett groaned. "Have a heart, Johnson! I'd like a little more than an hour's sleep!"

"It's 11:00, Garrett! Isn't the evidence hand-off supposed to be at noon? I need you to check the iPad to see if we have any updates from Andrews."

Garrett groaned again and pulled the pillow over his head.

Kelsey wormed her foot under his arm in an attempt to tickle him awake.

Garrett moved quickly, grabbing her leg and pulling her down on top of him. Rolling, he was soon on top of her, pinning her body beneath his.

He grinned. "You're losing it, Johnson. There's no way you should have fallen for that maneuver."

Kelsey looked up at him. "Well, I admit, I may be a bit compromised where you're concerned, at least at the moment."

She saw Garrett's eyes flicker to her lips, and she suspected he wanted to kiss her as much as she wanted him to.

"I also need your opinion on this dress," Kelsey said, forcing herself to complete the task at hand.

Garrett's eyes widened as he glanced down at the yellow bridesmaid dress she was wearing. "Well, why didn't you say so?" He said, rolling off of her and rising, while pulling her to her feet with him. "Who cares about the time or a message from Andrews. An opinion on a dress—now that's important."

Kelsey stood stiffly as Garrett circled around her, giving her the full inspection. Kelsey wasn't nearly as comfortable in a dress as she was jeans, and just the thought of a bridesmaid dress made her want to squirm. But she would wear a dress made of pizza boxes for Rachel. And in this case, Rachel had jumped out of a building with Kelsey's bridesmaid dress clutched in her hand, so Kelsey felt rather obligated to at least try it. And with the wedding fast approaching, she was on a deadline with a very impatient bride.

As she'd looked at the form-fitting, yellow gown in an upstairs mirror, she'd suddenly been plagued with self-doubt. The happy dress didn't seem to match her. While it was a perfect fit, she worried that she looked awkward, like she didn't belong. And that's when she'd decided to brave Garrett's opinion.

Now, as the length of his inspection stretched, she was again overwhelmed with doubt. What if she really did look terrible in Rachel's bridesmaid dress? As silly as it sounded, she certainly didn't want to mar Rachel's wedding in any way.

Having completed his full circle inspection, Kelsey felt Garrett behind her. His chest came against her back, and his arms wrapped around, his strong, calloused hands sliding along her own bare arms.

She felt his warm breath whispering in her ear. "Kelsey, you look beautiful. But since that is a very general statement, let me be more specific. "I

_____

like the way the dress hugs your hips and waist." His hands moved to slide from her hips up to her waist.

"I like the color. I think it makes you look brighter, happier. It makes your eyes sparkle, or is that just when you look at me?" He placed gentle kisses on her closed eyes. "It makes your coloring look all the more smooth, like china." He traced kisses along her jawline. "And your lips. Kelsey, for some reason, your dress makes your lips irresistible."

With a passion that equaled last night, Garrett finally claimed Kelsey's lips. But strangely, it was as if the kiss was the reverse. It started out fiery and passionate, with Kelsey feeling as if she couldn't get enough, desire coursing through both of them. But then, it calmed and grew deeper, more meaningful. It was no less passionate, but the slow way Garrett's mouth moved over hers spoke of emotion greater than the mere physical. There was a patience about it, a thorough enjoyment of something lasting and significant.

When Garrett's lips finally left her, there were tears in Kelsey's eyes, as if something profound had just happened, and yet she couldn't find a label to put on the emotion.

Garrett dragged in a breath. "I like your dress, Kelsey."

"I guess I should go change," Kelsey said quietly, not sure what to say. "I need to keep it nice for the wedding."

"That's a good idea. I'm not sure I could manage any coherent thought if you wore that all day."

Kelsey laughed and turned to the stairs. "I'll have to remember that."

Garrett headed toward the kitchen. "While you change, I'll see if Andrews left his place stocked with anything edible for breakfast."

Kelsey paused on the stairs. "Just to warn you, I don't cook," she said warily.

"You and I can both disarm multiple kinds of bombs; I'm sure we can figure it out."

"You don't have to eat a bomb," Kelsey grumbled, continuing the rest of the way up the stairs.

After returning to the kitchen, now in her jeans and leather jacket, Garrett stood staring blankly in front of the open refrigerator.

"No new messages from Andrews," he announced. "So I guess we follow the original plan for noon."

"That's unlike him," Kelsey said, worriedly.

"What do you mean?" Garrett asked, giving up on the refrigerator and pulling open cabinets instead.

"Given the situation, Andrews would be more likely to switch the plans multiple times in order to throw off anyone who may be on our trail."

"He could be concerned about the security issues of sending multiple messages," Garrett theorized, returning to the refrigerator.

"I guess," Kelsey said, though she wasn't convinced.

Garrett turned, a carton of eggs in his hand, "I'm not sure—"

Kelsey saw a red beam flash. Before her mind even registered what it was, she leapt for Garrett, knocking him down a fraction of a second before glass exploded with gunshots.

They covered their heads, hunkering down until the gunfire stopped. Then, into the silence, a friendly beep emitted from Garrett's tablet. He scrambled upright amidst the broken eggs and swiped his finger to unlock it. He read the message, and then handed it to Kelsey.

Mission compromised. Reports of a large unit of mercenaries headed your way. Not government agents. Fire at will.

"I guess we can shoot with a clear conscience," Kelsey surmised.

Garrett nodded. "Stay down!" he ordered, drawing his weapon.

"No! You stay down!" Kelsey hissed, her weapon already at the ready. She saw the mutiny in Garrett's eyes. "Matthews, if you want me to shoot this gun, you have to be behind me."

Understanding lit his eyes, and he reluctantly nodded. "Go get 'em."

Kelsey peered around the counter. After the initial barrage of gunfire, everything had gone eerily silent. "We have to wait until they breach," Kelsey said. "Otherwise we have no hope of hitting them."

Garrett nodded, handing her some extra ammo.

They waited, barely daring to breathe. A crash shook the house as multiple doors were broken simultaneously. Kelsey looked at Garrett and steadily counted for three seconds, then she stood and fired. She took out the two men closest first. Then she jumped sliding over the kitchen island feet first and knocking down the black-clad man on the other side while leaning back over her shoulder and shooting the man closest to the back door.

She heard Garrett shooting as well, and saw other men go down, but she didn't pay attention to his mode of attack.

Silence.

She turned around, seeing that all the attackers had been neutralized. She reached into her jacket and pulled out the package of evidence. "You need to go, Garrett. They are going to send in another wave. Let's head out the back and I'll cover you while you get the evidence out of here."

"You take the evidence," Garrett insisted. "Let me cover you."

"Matthews, we've been over this. The best way to protect me is to let me protect you. The evidence is safer with you. If I'm confronted directly, I'll lose it. But if I'm protecting you, we may have a chance of escaping with it."

"Fine," Garrett agreed. "But you'd better be right behind me."

Kelsey waited with her ear to the door, listening for any subtle creak that would indicate that the second wave was eminent. They needed to time it right so that their attackers were visible for neutralizing prior to opening the door.

She didn't hear a sound, but she suddenly felt a presence on the other side of the door. She yanked it open while Garrett stepped through, firing. Kelsey followed, quickly arranging herself in the front position and aiming for anything that moved.

It was broad daylight, but their assailants were all in camouflage. She tried not to think, focusing entirely on protecting Garrett and the evidence. They reached the tree line, and Kelsey moved to the rear. She let Garrett run ahead while she turned around, making sure they weren't attacked from the rear.

She saw movement and fired, instantly realizing that she'd just run out of ammo. Knowing that a quick escape was now the only option, she turned and ran. Trees flew past, but she was no longer sure which direction Garrett had taken.

She stumbled into a clearing. Before her were four men in camouflage, standing in a line with weapons aimed directly at her. She slid to a stop, immediately feeling the grip of awful fear. Heart pounding, muscles weak, she lifted her weapon and then bent to set it down in surrender.

"It looks like this is the end of the road, Agent Johnson," one of the men said, walking forward to search her for other weapons.

She saw her chance. As he searched her with one hand, he held his weapon loosely in his other hand. She knew that with one quick movement, she could have him on the ground, his weapon in her hands. In less than two seconds, she could then take out the other three men.

She tried, but she couldn't get her muscles to obey. They refused to perform the movements she knew would free her. And all because the other men still held a gun pointed at her.

Completely defeated, she didn't even fight back when she felt an arm go around her, stuffing something firmly over her mouth and nose.

She desperately hoped that Garrett had made it, but she had the awful feeling that he hadn't; that because of her actions, she had failed yet again.

Chapter 17

Kelsey awoke to darkness. In fact, she didn't even know for sure she was awake until she heard her name.

"Kelsey, are you awake?"

" Garrett, is that you? What happened? Where are we?"

"It's me. I don't know where we are. The last thing I remember, I was almost to the main road and a jeep pulled up to block me. I turned and felt something hit me in the back. A group of men surrounded me. I remember turning in a full circle and seeing you crumpled up in a seat in the jeep. Then I must have blacked out. They probably hit me with some kind of tranquilizer. The next thing I knew, I woke up here."

Kelsey's eyes gradually adjusted to the darkness, and she could see faint light from a vent in the top of the ceiling. She tried to move, but her hands were tied behind her. She tried twisting her hands, using the tricks she knew to try to get out of her bonds, but it was no use. It also didn't help that her hands throbbed in their bandages. She hadn't noticed the pain when firing her gun and trying to escape, but now she had to grit her teeth against it.

She sighed. "I assume you are tied up just as efficiently as I am?"

"I've managed to rub my wrists raw and get a little room, but I'd need a knife to get out. If we were tied with regular handcuffs, I might even be able to get out, but this rope is too tight."

"I have a pocketknife inside my boot," Kelsey said quickly. "It's hidden well, so they may not have found it."

She heard Garrett scooting her direction across the concrete floor. It took him a while, but as his hands finally connected with hers, she felt a thrill of comfort. Somehow she didn't feel quite so alone, and things didn't seem quite so desperate.

She slid and wiggled her right foot over to Garrett. Working himself into a crouching position, he hunched with his back toward her and slid his hands down her leg to meet her boot.

"Run your fingers right under the inside lip of the boot. There should be a small hidden pocket.

You might have to work to get the pocketknife out of its little sleeve."

Garrett's grunts were the only sound for several minutes, until finally, he fell back to the concrete and exclaimed, "I got it!"

"Do you think you can use it?" Kelsey asked anxiously.

"I think so, but it may take a while."

Kelsey was silent, wondering how much time they actually had before receiving visitors.

She felt Garrett move beside her so his back was up against the wall with hers. It helped to know he was close. She felt the warmth of his shoulder against hers, and he nudged her gently.

"Are you hurt?" he asked in concern.

"No, I'm fine. They used some kind of drug on me as well. But I gave up before they could do any real damage." Self-reproach dripped from her voice. "I assume the evidence is gone."

"Yes," Garrett acknowledged.

"So that means we have nothing. Even if we manage to escape, the vice president still wins, and we can't end this."

"Let's take one crisis at a time," Garrett said. "At least we're alive. We'll figure out our other options after we escape."

"Why *are* we alive?" Kelsey wondered. "After spending so much time and effort trying to kill us, why would they change their minds and decide to abduct us instead?"

"Something changed," Garrett surmised. "I'm sure they will still kill us, but they need something from us first. Remember, these aren't the same people who were after us before."

Kelsey thought. "The vice president was probably reaching her limit of dedicating government agents and resources without attracting attention. It would be difficult to indefinitely avoid questions with everything she was throwing at two relatively unimportant rogue agents."

"You're probably right. And if Andrews' messages were intercepted, she probably realized it wasn't just us who were onto her. There are definite advantages to hiring your own band of mercenary goons—a lot less questions and red tape."

"But that still doesn't answer the question of why they kept us alive."

"I'd rather not stick around to find out," Garrett grunted, adjusting again in his efforts.

Kelsey swallowed with difficulty. "We wouldn't be in this position if I hadn't lost my nerve. This is my fault."

"What happened?" Garrett asked gently.

Kelsey shrugged. "Exactly what all the psych reports said would happen. I couldn't make my body do what I needed in order to defend myself."

"Kelsey, you're being too hard on yourself. There were a lot of thugs with a lot of weapons. If you had fought back, you might have just succeeded in getting yourself killed."

"I had a chance," Kelsey confessed, self-reproach still straining her voice. " I could have at least tried. I saw the move I needed to make in order to disarm the guy closest to me and turn his weapon on the others. But I couldn't do it."

"You were fine right before that. You were pretty amazing back at the house. What happened?" There was no accusation in Garrett's voice, just compassion and curiosity.

"I wish I knew." Kelsey sighed and closed her eyes, forcing herself to relive that moment, trying to figure out what had happened. "I just froze. That's how this thing works. It's happened before, and it is the reason I can never be trusted in the field."

"Do you recall what you were thinking right before you froze?"

Kelsey groaned. She knew Garrett was trying to be helpful, but he was definitely not succeeding! "For Pete's sake, Garrett! Don't try to psychoanalyze me! Many who are much more qualified than you have tried and failed!"

Garrett shifted so he faced her fully in the darkness. "I'm not trying to psychoanalyze you, Kelsey! I'm trying to figure out how best to convince you that by protecting yourself, you protect others."

"Well, clearly that was the case this time," Kelsey said dryly. "If I hadn't gotten caught, maybe you wouldn't have. But in the moment when I had multiple guns aimed at me, I didn't really analyze all potential ramifications."

"That's not what I'm talking about, Kelsey." Garrett's voice was not harsh, but it was firm. "I can't stand the thought of something happening to you. I'm sure your mother can't either. You are valuable and important to so many people. What would Rachel do without her best friend? Maybe the root of your issue is that you see the value in others so much more than in yourself. But by not protecting yourself, you're not protecting them. For those who love you, losing you would be worse than physical injury."

Kelsey was silent. She didn't want to admit that Garrett may be right. She didn't have much self-worth. How could she after what she'd done to her father?

In the silence, Kelsey became aware of the steady drip of water. Cold seeped into her from the concrete beneath and behind her. And still she wasn't any closer to any true epiphany. Even if Garrett was right, how did she convince herself of her own worth.

"Kelsey, you are important," Garrett said, finally interrupting her thoughts. "You are valuable. God created you. He loves you. He values you. When you fight, don't think of fighting for yourself. Protect yourself in the name of God, because you are His child, and for the sake of those who love you."

Without fully understanding why, a sob caught in her throat, and Garrett's arms came around her. He caught her close, whispering, "I want you to protect yourself, but for my sake. I want to know you'll fight with the same tenacity you do for others, because I can't handle the thought of something happening to you. Kelsey, I—"

Kelsey cut him off, quickly pulling back. " Garrett, don't say something you'll regret when all of this is over. The past forty-eight hours don't put either of us in a good mindset to be declaring feelings one way or another. Remember, before two days ago, you didn't even like me!"

"Kelsey, would you please stop saying that," Garrett sputtered. "First of all, that is simply not true! You said I disliked you from the first day. Actually, the problem was that I liked you way too much!"

"What are you talking about?"

"You aren't the only one with issues, Kelsey Johnson. I've avoided commitment for a very long time. I usually date women who I have no chance of really falling for and being serious about. I've been interested in a good time, and that's about it. Yes, I fell for Rachel, but if you think about it, even she was unattainable. I fell for a woman who was already in love with another guy. However, from the first day I saw you, you scared me. I never asked you out because I already liked you way too much. I knew if we ever dated, that it would be serious, and I wasn't ready for that. So I've spent the last few years desperately trying to dislike you and make up for the fact that I pretty much fell hard at first sight."

"That's why you dated the entire Department of Homeland Security, except me?" Kelsey asked, incredulous.

"Yes," Garrett replied, his tone achingly honest. "And I was obviously correct. Kissing you last night completely ruined me for ever wanting to kiss another woman. Kelsey, the way I feel is not a new thing; it's me finally coming to terms with the fact that you're the only one I want."

Gently, he reached out and caressed her face.

"You're such a jerk, Garrett Matthews! Do you know how much I've hated myself for being hopelessly attracted to—"

Garrett kissed her. Once again, Kelsey's heart thumped wildly and she realized again that she'd never felt this way about any other man.

He ran his fingers through her hair. She longed to wrap her arms around him, but she couldn't with her hands tied behind her—"

" Garrett, you're free!" she said, jerking away. "What are you doing?" Realizing that he'd actually been free for the last few minutes caused her anger to rise. "We should be trying to escape and you're here—"

"Romancing my girl?" he finished. "Yes, that's exactly what I'm doing. Now, if you're clear on where we stand, turn around so I can cut through your rope."

Kelsey masked the thrill of pleasure at his words and obediently maneuvered to give Garrett access to her entrapped hands.

Silence stretched. Kelsey didn't want to distract his concentration, but after several minutes, she questioned worriedly, "Is there a problem?" It certainly didn't feel like he was making any progress.

"Yes," he replied. "Your pocketknife broke before I was free. Fortunately, I'd sawed through my ropes enough that I was able to pull them the rest of the way apart. But the blade itself broke. I'm trying to use the pieces to cut through yours, but it isn't working. There isn't enough of a blade left."

Kelsey swallowed. "What are our escape options. My legs aren't tied, maybe I can just follow if you blaze the way."

"I think the only door to this cell is dead bolted from the outside. I see our only escape route as up through the vent."

Kelsey looked up to the dim light filtering through the vent overhead. It looked like a fairly simple task to remove the metal grill, with plenty of room for a person to pull himself through, though she had no idea where the vent may lead.

Feeling like their time was running out, Kelsey spoke quickly. " Garrett, this is pointless. That is a one person escape route anyway. We're just wasting time, since it would do me no good to be free. One of us will have to stand on the shoulders of the other in order to reach the vent. There's no way for the other person to get through."

"I'm not leaving you!" Garrett grunted.

"Yes, you are!" Kelsey insisted. "Your only chance of saving me is to escape and find help. If you don't leave now, we'll both be stuck here."

Garrett's frantic movements finally stopped.

The sound of footsteps echoed to their ears. "Hurry, Garrett! Go now!"

Garrett helped Kelsey to her feet, and she positioned herself beneath the vent. She waited, knowing that Garrett using her for a step stool was going to hurt.

But instead of feeling his weight, she felt his finger tip her chin up.

"Kelsey, promise me you'll fight. If not for yourself, then for me."

Kelsey opened her mouth to reply, but now voices joined the footsteps outside the cell.

Garrett quickly slipped behind her. Stepping first on her bound wrists, he boosted himself to her shoulders.

Kelsey breathed deeply, trying to remove her thoughts to a place where a man likely twice her weight wasn't standing on her shoulders.

The whole process took less than five seconds, and Garrett's weight was gone as he lifted himself into the open vent. "Promise me!" he whispered fiercely before carefully replacing the grill for the vent. The last thing she heard from him was the sound of his desperate whispered prayer, "God, please keep her safe!"

Then he was gone.

And the door to her cell opened.

Chapter 18

"Where is he?" the man growled.

Kelsey remained mute, staring off into space with a blank expression.

Her antagonist took two steps and smacked her across the face with the back of his hand. "I said, 'Where is he?'"

Despite the taste of blood on her lips, Kelsey kept her silence.

A deep animalistic grown erupted from the man's chest, and Kelsey braced herself for another onslaught.

"There's no sense wasting time," another man said, speaking up from near the door with a bored tone. "What do we care if the guy pulled a Houdini and disappeared? Rohan only needed the woman anyway."

The third man spoke up from the shadows. "He's right. Let's get her down there. If Rohan wants her to talk, let him be the one to get it out of her."

The first man grabbed her arm roughly and pulled her to her feet.

Before she could get her balance, she was being dragged out of the cell and down a dark hallway, lit only by dim, impotent lights spaced sparsely along the sides. Though her feet tripped, her captors still dragged her. With her hands still secured behind her back and three armed men surrounding her, she felt an awful sense of helplessness overwhelm her. She had no idea where they were going, but she dreaded what awaited her.

Please hurry, Garrett! She thought, desperately wishing her cry would somehow reach her would-be rescuer. But she knew the chances of Garrett escaping cleanly were slim, and the chances of him returning, especially before she met whatever fate awaited, were even less likely.

She didn't know who this Rohan person was, or what he needed from her, but the mere mention of his name had chilled her. She was trained to withstand torture; she wasn't really worried about that. However, she was worried about if her body would play the traitor yet again and refuse to defend herself.

One of the men opened a loudly screeching metal door, and another one at her back pushed her through roughly. Kelsey stumbled and fell, her cheek slamming against the hard floor. Ignoring the pain, Kelsey blinked in the harsh light, the glare a stark contrast to the hall. Instead of concrete, her face was pressed against white linoleum. She slowly rolled and drew herself up, taking the time to study her surroundings, which were all the more shocking when compared to the environment she'd just exited.

Her gaze bounced from bright, overhead lights to computers sitting on a well-organized desk. A printer stood in a corner, and Kelsey recognized several other pieces of rather impressive technology. She appeared to be in a well-equipped office.

"There was no sign of the other prisoner," one of the men reported.

"I wouldn't expect there to be," responded a wheezy voice. A man in a suit stood from where he'd been sitting in a high-backed leather chair in front of the computers. "I have men on it. But, for now, we need to deal with the business at hand."

He turned to Kelsey. His eyes met hers in a rather mocking way, as if he was taking her measure.

He was an older man who had not a single strand of hair on is bald head. With a pair of thick glasses perched on his nose, he almost appeared to be a stereotypical businessman. He wasn't tall, but from what Kelsey saw with her few quick glances, she realized he commanded the respect, and even fear, of the other men. This must be Rohan.

He went behind Kelsey and untied her wrists. "Please sit," he said, gesturing to a chair on wheels perched in front of a computer. His tone was casual and friendly, as if Kelsey was a welcome visitor in his home.

Grateful to at least have her arms free, she rubbed her sore wrists, even as her mind hopelessly worked on methods of escape. Unfortunately, she knew there were none.

"I'd rather stand," Kelsey bit back, not wanting to bother with any potential mind games.

"That's fine." Rohan nodded, unfazed. "Since I see you'd rather forgo any pleasantries, I'll get right to the point. I'm familiar with your profile. With your skills and knowledge, you shouldn't find it too difficult to hack into a few secure government agencies. Here is a list of three agencies and call numbers for files that need to be removed from each."

Pieces clicked into place, and Kelsey suddenly understood both why she was alive and why Rohan didn't seem to be overly concerned about Garrett's disappearance. She was the one with technology expertise. If Rohan was familiar with her dossier, then he knew that, if there was a difficult technological problem no one else could solve, Kelsey was the one assigned to the task.

"No," Kelsey answered flatly, her voice firm.

At a subtle nod from Rohan, two of the camouflaged thugs grabbed her roughly and shoved her into the chair facing the computer.

With a chilling click, Rohan ground the barrel of a gun into Kelsey's temple.

"You see," he hissed in her ear, all trace of good humor gone. "I read *all* of your profile, even the parts Andrews took great pains to hide."

Chills raced down Kelsey's spine.

"I really need you to break into those sites, Miss Johnson, and if you refuse to do it, you are of no use to me. I have no problem putting a bullet in your brain, but I hope that simple fact might provide the psychological incentive for your fingers to get busy on that keyboard."

Kelsey swallowed with difficulty. Sweat beaded across her forehead. If he'd read even the sealed files, then he knew her entire history and would not hesitate to use it against her, exactly what Andrews had wanted to prevent by keeping her background hidden. But the cold barrel of a gun pressed to her temple confirmed their worst fears had come true.

A wave of helplessness washed over her. Though she hated it and begged herself not to do so, her traitorous fingers obediently perched on the keyboard and began typing.

"Good girl," Rohan sneered. "We will leave you to your work. Know that we have cameras on you. If you get out of the chair or try anything, rest assured there will be no further talk, instructions, or negotiations. You will be greeted with a bullet to the head."

Rohan turned to the other men. "Now let's see to the issue of our escaped loose end."

The men left with a click of the door closing, and Kelsey stared at the computer screen, her eyes filling with tears.

How could she betray her country and everything she knew to be right? In her head, she could easily say that she would rather die than do what Rohan demanded. And yet, she knew her body wouldn't cooperate.

She didn't want to do this! She didn't want to provide assistance to an enemy who planned untold crimes.

Her heart aching painfully, Kelsey shut her eyes, the sheer horror of the situation completely overwhelming her.

God help me! She cried in complete desperation.

But that one cry, flung out more to the universe, seemed to open a door. And she had the immediate sensation that there was a person standing behind it.

Everything Garrett had said came back in a rush. Had her horrible past had a purpose? She could never believe that a good God could have *wanted* something like that to happen to a young girl. But even if that evil had saddened him, couldn't He have still used if for something good?

Redemption, wasn't that the word? She had spent so much time believing that she wasn't worth fighting for, wasn't worth redeeming. But Garrett had seemed to think otherwise. His words floated as if filtering down from the vents in the room.

Kelsey, you are important. You are valuable. God created you. He loves you. He values you. When you fight, don't think of fighting for yourself,. Protect yourself in the name of God, because you are His child, and for the sake of those who love you.

Tears spilled out and coursed down her face. Sobs choked, and her hands, still positioned over the keyboard, trembled.

God, please forgive me! I know I don't deserve your love or forgiveness. I've spent most of my life doing what I wanted and denying you. I'm tired of doing this on my own! I want to belong to you! Please save me in every sense. Save me through Jesus's death paying for my sins, and save me from myself. My life is yours. Make me who you want me to be.

Then the strangest thing happened. It was as if the person standing in the door came out and wrapped His arms around Kelsey. She felt a wholeness and a sense of belonging like she'd never before felt.

"Miss Johnson," Kelsey jumped at the sound of the speaker in the corner belching to life. "I don't mean to rush you, but it certainly doesn't appear you're getting any work done. My patience is running rather thin. If you can't do this in a timely manner, I will pursue other options and get rid of the excess."

"Understood," Kelsey promptly replied, her training covering when her emotions were failing. "Please realize that I have to do things very strategically if you want files deleted quickly and without attracting attention. I need to have my plan in place prior to making the hack."

"Then think quickly," Rohan hissed. "You're on a timer with your life expiring at the buzzer."

The speaker fell silent.

Kelsey took deep breaths, trying to recapture the moment she'd had before the interruption. She'd wanted to stay there forever, to never leave that feeling of being wrapped in God's arms. Yet Rohan's voice had stolen it away with the reminder of her current situation. Strangely, she still felt different somehow, like the presence that was with her had not been snatched away after all. With a sense of awe at her newfound faith, Kelsey realized that she was not alone. Now and forever, she would have Someone by her side who was bigger than any impossible situation she had to face.

Lord, please get me out of here and give me the strength to do as Garrett said—to fight for You and a purpose greater than myself, to defend myself when I must, because I am loved by You and others.

With new determination, Kelsey opened her eyes and looked at the screen in front of her. All hesitation and uncertainty was gone. She knew she couldn't do what was wrong, no matter what. She couldn't hack those sites and delete the evidence that would provide assistance for potential terrorists.

But she also knew her predicament seemed completely impossible. She was trapped in a facility filled with enemy agents, and she had no doubt Rohan would follow through on his threat to kill her. So was she fated to soon meet the God she had just put her faith in, or was there any hope that she could escape with her life?

Kelsey spent several minutes wasting time, trying to think of a way out. She visited each of the sites, pretending to scout around in preparation for the hack. But try as she might, she couldn't think of a single plan that allowed her to not perform the hack and live to tell about it.

Idly, she stared down at her fingers perched on the keyboard. Her gaze caught on the "print screen" key, and a memory burst through her mind.

She had been thinking inside the box this entire time. But she knew better! She'd known that when her first day had included a printer that wouldn't print a required assignment.

What do you do when given an impossible task? You change the color of the ink!

Kelsey quickly began typing, the plan still forming as she started assembling what she would need. She wouldn't have time to program everything she needed, so she quickly hacked into Homeland Security, which thankfully was one of the agencies on the list. But the first thing she did was pull one of her own projects up.

It took a lot of work, and she realized what she was doing was very dangerous. Her only hope was that those monitoring her would not be savvy enough to track her every movement, or analyze each strand of code she rapidly wrote.

After at least two hours, the door to the room clicked open, and Rohan and two of his armed goons entered.

Her time was up. If they had any clue of what she had done, she would be killed. She was savvy enough to realize that, even if they thought she'd been successful in her assignment, she would still likely be killed. A completed task meant they would have no further use for her. Either way, this was the moment when she would have to, with God's help, overcome her own psychological problems to defend her life and fight her way out of this room.

"I believe you were successful in hacking into the three sites?" Rohan questioned.

"Yes," Kelsey confirmed. "I took screenshots of each file prior to deleting it. I saved the files in a folder on the desktop."

"Yes, we saw that," Rohand confirmed. He casually walked over to her side, leaning over to look at her screen.

The two other men fanned out behind her desk chair.

"Your work seemed to greatly impress those I had monitoring you. They admitted they couldn't follow everything you did. While I was hoping you'd complete the task sooner, they assured me it was done in a timely manner, and that the hacks were not immediately detected by the agencies."

Kelsey nodded, not knowing what to say. She sat facing forward in the chair, looking at him warily out of the corner of her eye.

"So if that is all true, why do I still not trust you?" Rohan said, his tone musing thoughtfully. He shrugged. "I guess it doesn't matter. You've proven yourself to be cooperative in small things." He pulled out his gun and placed it to her head once again. "Now I'm going to need you to do a little bit bigger job for me."

Chapter 19

Kelsey's throat constricted, and she felt her body's same traitorous reaction that would prevent her from defending herself

God help me! she breathed, knowing the next few seconds would be the test that determined the course for her life.

Her gaze flickered down to the bottom of the screen, where a green bar had marked the progress of the upload she had started prior to Rohan entering. It now read, "Completed."

Kelsey felt the gun at her temple and tasted the fear. Her body shook with its desire to fold to whatever demands were made. And yet, despite the fear, the uncertainty, and haunting memories that gripped her tightly…

Kelsey spun around in the swiveling chair, right as her left arm swung up, knocking the barrel of Rohan's gun with the side of her hand. Coming up off the chair, her foot snapped up in a swift kick to the groin. Rohan bent over in pain, and Kelsey grabbed his wrist, twisting it to the point that the tendons or bones would surely snap. He gasped in pain, and his weapon clattered to the floor. Catching movement from the corner of her eye, she quickly landed a blow to Rohan's temple with her fist.

The movement brought Rohan down, but also knocked the blisters beneath the bandages on her hand, rubbing the raw skin and shooting intense pain all the way up her arm.

At the same time, the man directly in back of the chair lunged forward. Kelsey saw the movement, but without time to pick up Rohan's gun, she slid it across the floor with her foot and then met her attacker with a side kick that landed on target, directly in the chest. The man gasped and stopped as if immediately frozen. With a quick crescent kick to the head, he fell over unconscious.

Her foot never landed from the kick. Instead, she swung it back with a swift, hard blow, sending the office chair careening into the third man. He staggered back, but didn't go down. Kelsey took two steps and jumped, knocking the man's jaw up with a snap kick. Yet he still didn't go down. Like an angry bull, he came after her, grabbing at her before he'd even regained his balance. Kelsey leapt away, but barely. Grabbing the office chair, she threw it at him. It was a direct hit. He dropped to the floor.

Now her last move may not have been a Rachel-approved karate move, but at least she'd gotten the job done.

Breathing heavily from adrenaline and exertion, Kelsey swiftly clambered over him, searched through the man's pockets to locate the same pair of handcuffs that had been used to tie her up, and cuffed him to a leg of the desk. While not quite unconscious, he was groaning. But, with the hefty partner of a desk, he wasn't going anywhere soon.

Turning, Kelsey assessed the rest of the scene. The second guy was sprawled where he had landed, and he would to be unconscious for a while.

Kelsey gathered all the weapons she could find on the nearest two men. After stuffing the guns in her jacket, waistband, and everywhere else she could, she stepped over the unconscious man and picked up Rohan's gun where it still lay on the floor.

"You'll never make it out of here alive," Rohan groaned from the floor, cradling his injured wrist close to his body.

Reaching down, she grabbed the collar of Rohan's suit, pulling him to his feet despite the pain shooting through her hands.

"If I don't, you don't," she said, quickly searching him for any other weapons. When she found nothing, she pushed him to the door in front of her. "You'll make a nice shield. Besides, I think our chances are decent. You have some very helpful facility maps in your database."

Rohan shot her a look of pure hatred. "That's impossible," he spat. "Your every move was monitored. I would have known if you'd accessed anything like documents in our system."

Not willing to waste any valuable time, Kelsey pushed Rohan out the door, even as she spoke. "I won't bore you with the details, but I created a dummy system, a façade for you to see what you wanted to see while I did what I wanted to do behind it. I then hacked into your own system and got busy while all my actions on the façade layer appeared to complete your assigned tasks.

"So you never hacked into any of the government agencies?" Rohan asked.

"Well, I pretended to."

"You couldn't have set up an elaborate system that quickly," he protested, derision and disbelief vying for dominance in his tone.

Kelsey was silent, thinking that she was done talking to Rohan. They were nearing a corner that would require her full attention to navigate. Besides, Rohan didn't know the specifics of how she had managed her task. He didn't need to know that she actually did hack into one government site— Homeland Security. Or that she had accessed her own projects, specifically the project she had created for intelligence purposes. It was a program that created a dummy system in which the operator could work undetected behind a screen. With a few adjustments, Kelsey was able to adapt the screen to show the requested actions, and then monitor both the actual and perceived actions. Though this was the first time she'd used the program in the field, the project she'd dubbed, "The Wizard of Oz," had performed beautifully, and Rohan's confusion was the proof.

She only hoped that the information she had uploaded from this system to Homeland Security had been received and would be the evidence they needed. If the task had completed, then the whole mess would be over. The outcome would no longer depend on her. Even if she didn't make it out of here, she would have still succeeded in saving Garrett and bringing down a very powerful man and his ring of corruption.

But she fully intended to try to live.

They got to the corner, and Kelsey urged Rohan forward, whispering. "You go first."

"You are under the mistaken impression that they will care if they shoot me!" Rohan hissed. "They won't. Now that we have been compromised, I will be eliminated. I have no authority now. The security cameras in the office were live; they already know you've escaped, and are closing in on our location. Yet, at any second, my boss might just decide to cut his losses and bomb the whole place and everyone in it."

"I'm not counting on your value as a hostage," Kelsey retorted. "I value you as a shield or a decoy to draw their fire. Now move!"

Rohan stumbled into the intersection. Kelsey was right behind him, with weapon up, sweeping the empty hall. When she was confident it was clear, she urged Rohan to the stairs. This was the most dangerous part of the escape. From the maps, she knew that they were in a subterranean level, approximately three stories down from the ground floor. The elevators would be shut down immediately following her escape, which meant the only option was the stairs. It put her in a weak position to be climbing the stairs. If someone stood at the top, they could shoot and she would have nowhere to go.

Knowing it was her only chance, she found the fuse box exactly where the building schematics had shown. She swung open the metal door and, using the butt of her gun, she smashed it repeatedly as hard as she could. The force vibrated through her whole body, and she bit her lip to keep from crying out with the pain from her hands. Pieces of plastic and metal dropped from the box, and then the lights went black.

"Go," she told Rohan, pushing him up the stairs before her.

"How am I supposed to see?" he grumbled.

"With your feet!" Kelsey ordered. "At least until your eyes adjust. Move."

Kelsey swallowed. They had to make it up three levels to the ground floor. Her heart pounded. She knew how risky this was.

She kept her hand on the rail. There was virtually no light for which her eyes could adjust in the pitch black. But if she couldn't see them, hopefully, they couldn't see her.

Kelsey counted the steps.

First floor.

Second floor.

One more to go. But even if she made it to the ground level, she knew she wouldn't be safe. The simple fact that they hadn't met any resistance told her that they were simply waiting for her. They were preparing an ambush.

Kelsey paused at the landing to the ground level. There was only one door. Once they opened it, they would be moving from the black stairwell into a fully-lit hallway. She knew the fuse box she'd destroyed had only controlled electricity on the lower levels. She also knew that if she was planning an ambush, this is where it would happen. There was no sense risking a fight on the stairwell where shots could ricochet. Better to wait until she opened the door to find an arsenal of weapons aimed at her.

"Open the door, and then get out of the way," Kelsey instructed Rohan, readying herself in position at the other side of the door. She arranged all of her weapons for easy access. When Rohan swung open the door, she would wait for the initial shots, then shoot everything she could.

Kelsey called softly, "Three. Two. One."

Rohan opened the door, but instead of moving to the side as she'd instructed, he hesitated.

The gunfire was instant. The door opened fully, the shaft of light spotlighting Rohan as bullets ripped into his body, knocking him backward.

Something clicked in Kelsey's mind and all fear vanished.

She stepped through the doorway. Two hallways came to a T at the entrance to the stairs The light was blinding, but before a split second had passed, she somehow knew that there were at least three attackers, all coming from the three different directions of the hallways.

Kelsey hurled herself forward. With a gun in each hand, she shot continuously, forward, left and right. She moved so quickly, she was firing before the attackers realized she was through the door.

After single shots to the left and right, she was past the side hallways and moving ahead. Multiple men dropped before her, and still she kept firing.

She heard gunshots from behind, and something knocked her left shoulder hard. She immediately dropped and swept her foot around, pivoting to the opposite direction. She shot two men coming up behind her.

Stepping forward, she turned back around to see two more men turning a corner. She knew they had the advantage with her eyes still blurred and watery as they adjusted to the light. She needed to get closer.

Taking a running two steps, she leapt over the pile of bodies crowding the hallway and tucked herself into a roll. She barely felt the floor before springing up and firing three feet from the men.

She shot the one on her right.

The other one drew his weapon up. She grabbed it, forcing it down as she snapped a kick to the groin.

The weapon went off.

With the force of Kelsey's groin kick, the man's head bent low. Kelsey landed an elbow to the face and then a hand chop to his neck. He dropped.

Breathing hard, Kelsey turned, weapon at the ready.

Her gaze flashed around. She turned. Looking. Listening.

But everything was silent, her quick breaths the only sound in a hallway littered with multiple men sprawled across the floor.

Quickly, she checked each camouflaged body, careful to not turn her back on anyone who might still do her harm. With her quick assessment, she was confident that everyone was dead, unconscious, or in such bad shape, they wouldn't be bothering her.

Still, Kelsey disarmed the few who were still alive, and tried not to think about what had just happened. The scene where she now found herself might haunt her nightmares, but for now, she turned her emotions off like the trained agent she was, knowing that she still needed to make it out alive.

She looked up, back toward the door still open to the stairs, and she met a pair of eyes. But they weren't lifeless and staring. They were instead calmly watching her every move.

Rohan was still alive, though immobile with his back against the cement wall of the stairway, exactly where he had fallen after the initial barrage of bullets.

Kelsey hurried to him, realizing quickly that, though his eyes were clear, the shadow of death was creeping near, and there was nothing she could do to chase it away. She knelt down, her gaze tracing the multiple bullet wounds in his chest. It was amazing that he was still alive. Though his pallor and the shaking of his body told her that the end was near.

"I'm sorry… " Kelsey started, but she didn't even know what she was apologizing for. He'd been shot by his own men, exactly as he'd feared. This was an evil man who would not hesitate to kill her. Yet death was the great equalizer, and it seemed something should be said.

"The report lied," he coughed out, his eyes fixed on her. "It said you were psychologically incapable of defending yourself. I've never seen anyone do what you just did. At least ten men... Less than a minute... Defending no one but... you." His voice grew so weak that the last word was simply mouthed, with no sound brushing past his white lips.

"It didn't lie," Kelsey answered. "I had help."

Rohan's eyebrows raised a fraction, as if posing a question he could not voice.

"God," Kelsey whispered, the soft sound in contrast to the firm conviction in her tone.

A light flashed through Rohan's eyes, almost as if he suddenly remembered something. Then the light faded and the muscles in his face relaxed.

Kelsey saw the pulse in his neck beat one last time, and then the utter stillness of death wrapped Rohan in its shroud.

Kelsey stood, and without a backward glance, quickly made her way through the labyrinth of hallways to where she knew she should find the front entrance. She'd hoped that they had sent all of their men at her at once, but she held her weapons ready, checking each corner before turning.

She heard a voice and slowed. From the facility maps, she knew she should be getting close to the front security area.

"Guys, we need some help out here! There are multiple threats showing on our security feed!"

Kelsey slowly crept forward. Peering into the security area, she saw two men facing a wall of security screens with their backs to her.

After the beat of several seconds, the voice spoke again. "Come on, people! She's one woman! We need people up here now! We're going to be raided!"

Kelsey focused on the man who was not speaking. Remembering a nerve strike Rachel showed her once, she sent a quick blow to his temple, followed by a precise hit to the carotid artery in the neck. He immediately slumped in his chair, never realizing what had happened. With a swift kick to the wheeled office chair, Kelsey sent him out of the way and sliding across the tiled floor.

Before the chair wheeled to a stop, Kelsey had her gun pressed to the other man's head. "Open the doors," she demanded calmly.

"Ummm... I.... a..." the man stuttered, as if English was suddenly a foreign language.

Kelsey watched as his eyes darted back to his communication system, as if hoping it would squawk to life and offer rescue.

"They aren't coming," Kelsey assured. "You must have been distracted. Go ahead, check the security cameras around the stairs to the lower level."

Kelsey moved the gun slightly to allow him to turn and push a button. She watched his eyes widen as he frantically switched through all of the cameras, each showing nothing but his comrades cluttering the hallway floor.

"What...? How...?" He turned and looked behind Kelsey, as if expecting to see an army behind her.

"Just me." Kelsey said softly. "But since I took out all of your buddies, I would say you are severely outnumbered."

Kelsey watched fear spark in the man's eyes. He nervously wet his lips and swallowed repeatedly.

When she was sure the poor man was at his breaking point, she once again made her demand, slowly enunciating each word. "Open. The. Door."

The man nodded and quickly turned to obey.

A door slid open, and he turned back to Kelsey, cowering in fear.

Seeing extension cords beneath his work station, Kelsey bent, pulling at and unplugging them. Then she tied his hands and feet, looping the cord repeatedly through the chair to secure him tightly. Finished, she wheeled him to the other side of the room where he had no hope of reaching his control panel or anything else useful.

"Thank you," the man said repeatedly, his expression relieved.

While Kelsey found it amusing that the man kept thanking her for tying him up, he obviously feared he would end up like his comrades in the hall. Fortunately for him, Kelsey wasn't in the habit of incapacitating those who weren't trying to kill her.

Assuring herself that the other security guard was still unconscious, Kelsey quickly walked through the open sliding door and into a darkened warehouse. This was apparently the front façade to a secret building. With the sliding doors shut, anyone walking in from the outside would assume it was an old, abandoned warehouse.

Kelsey walked toward the dull grimy windows along the front. Her boots echoed on the concrete of the large, empty space. Finding a door, Kelsey unlatched the lock and swung the creaking hinges wide.

The waning sunlight momentarily blinded Kelsey as she stumbled out the door into the fresh air. Eager to be away from this place, she kept walking even before her vision cleared. After about ten steps, she turned and looked back at where she'd come. A dilapidated building rose behind her, blending in unremarkably with the surrounding old buildings.

New York. Kelsey had grown up in an area similar to this, a part of the city that had been forgotten by those with money to invest elsewhere. Seeing the similar stained concrete, forlorn buildings, and rickety fire escapes that provided more danger than safety, she was fairly certain that whoever these mercenaries were, they had made their hideout in New York.

Feeling dizzy, Kelsey turned around, her now clear gaze performing an automatic surveillance of her surroundings.

She froze.

Her heart leapt into her throat.

She counted three. Three snipers with weapons trained on her.

Chapter 20

Slowly, with hands fully visible away from her body, Kelsey turned a full circle.

There were probably more than three. Part of a sniper's job was remaining hidden. The only reason she could spot them is that she knew what to look for in the buildings around her.

"Hold!" A voice called. "That's Agent Johnson!"

Then a man emerged from the shadows of a building. He came toward her, sprinting over debris and crushed concrete that had once had a purpose.

At some point, she realized it was Garrett. But everything had a rather dream-like quality to it, as if he was there, but not really.

Garrett stopped short of touching her, the look on his face cautious and almost horrified as she watched his eyes flash from her head to her feet.

"I need an ambulance," he said urgently. "Right now."

Kelsey realized he was speaking into his earpiece, but the fact that the order wasn't directed at her didn't stop the panic.

"What's wrong?" she demanded, scanning him for injury. "Where are you hurt?"

"I'm fine," Garrett said, "But you—"

"What's wrong?" Kelsey persisted. "You were supposed to get away! Why are you even here?"

"I'm here to rescue you!" Garrett shot back, the corner of his mouth quirking up in an expression of irony. "Obviously, that wasn't necessary."

Kelsey shook her head, trying to clear away the fog. She felt herself sway, and she blinked, trying to keep hold of the dream.

"Kelsey, can I have the gun?" Garrett asked softly.

"Which one?" Kelsey asked, her eyes flying wide as she thrust a gun toward Garrett, drew one of her many spares, and turned to meet whatever danger would require a gun.

"Never mind," Garrett muttered, running a hand through his hair. "Kelsey, I think the coast is clear. I have men positioned to cover us from every angle. But if I don't fully disarm you, will you promise not to shoot or otherwise maim me when I pick you up to carry you out of here?"

"Why would you do that? Kelsey asked, completely flabbergasted.

"Kelsey, you've been shot. At least twice. Haven't you noticed the massive amount of blood? And since you're about to pass out from shock and blood loss, I'm going to carry you to the ambulance."

Kelsey's mind struggled to keep up with Garrett's words. But he was speaking too fast. And she felt as if her thoughts were wading through mud.

Did he say something about blood? Kelsey looked down at herself. Gingerly, she felt her side, then held up blood-smeared fingers. But that couldn't be her blood.

The world swayed.

Garrett, caught her and carefully swung her up into his arms, weapons and all. "I'll take my chances," Garrett muttered as he started walking over the rubble. "Play nice, Snow White. I'm just trying to help you."

"I don't need you to rescue me," Kelsey said, her mind focusing on what he'd said earlier.

"I wouldn't dream of it," Garrett responded, walking quickly, with Kelsey's weight seeming to be no more burden than a rag doll. "You obviously took care of that yourself."

"I didn't do it myself," Kelsey murmured, closing her eyes against the dizziness. "I think God was the one who did the rescuing."

Kelsey's head fell against Garrett's shoulder, and though she didn't lose consciousness, she couldn't seem to make her mouth form any more words. She wanted to tell Garrett everything that had happened. She also wanted to tell him how nice his arms felt.

It was okay to let him hold her, just this once, right?

Kelsey opened her eyes to the flashing lights of an ambulance, and Garrett gently laid her on a gurney. He climbed up beside her, and with the slamming of the ambulance doors, they were off with sirens wailing.

She felt pricks and nudges, as the ambulance medics did their work. She was also aware of Garrett removing all of her weapons, even the ones in her waistband, pockets, and boot.

She couldn't figure out why everyone was looking so grim, and she really wished they would shut off that infernal siren.

One of the paramedics glanced up at Kelsey's face. "I don't understand how she's still conscious," he muttered to his colleague, as if Kelsey's hearing had blacked out, even if the rest of her hadn't.

When the ambulance stopped, Kelsey was pulled out and wheeled into a hospital. Faces swirled around her, their voices blending together in an unintelligible mash. She was awake through all the prodding, her gaze frantically searching for Garrett among the kaleidoscope of faces.

"Kelsey, they are going to take you to surgery now." Garrett's face shone above her, backlit against the hospital's fluorescent lights.

Kelsey frantically grabbed for Garrett's hand. She didn't want surgery! Everyone looked so grim. What if she didn't come out?

"It's okay," Garrett soothed, gently brushing her hair off her forehead. "You're going to be fine, and I'll be right here when you wake up." Before she could protest, she was wheeled into a different room, and people with blue caps and masks put a plastic contraption over her mouth and nose.

Someone was counting, like the countdown to the launch of a rocket.

Kelsey mentally counted with him. She didn't know why it mattered, but she wanted to make it to 1. But before the countdown reached the end, the number 1 disappeared.

Kelsey listened a long time, waiting for that final number, wondering where it had gone, but all she could hear was a steady beep.

She turned her head and pain radiated to her left shoulder and down her right side.

"Hold still, Kelsey," a familiar voice instructed. "You're out of surgery. Everything is fine. Stay still and take your time waking up."

" Garrett... " Kelsey groaned, her voice dry and scratchy. She fought against the strands of sleep drawing her back in, but she couldn't open her eyes to grasp more than a few brief instants of light.

She felt Garrett's warm hand holding hers and a gentle touch on her cheek.

"I'm here and I'm not going anywhere. Just relax."

Kelsey reluctantly let sleep pull her back down, too exhausted to fight.

The next time she awoke was much easier. Her eyes blinked open, and she saw Garrett sitting right beside her bed. His head was back and his eyes were closed. He looked haggard.

She didn't want to wake him, but his eyes flashed open anyway.

"Hi," he said with a gentle smile. "How are you feeling?"

"You tell me," she rasped out.

Garrett quickly retrieved a cup with a straw and held it so she could sip the ice water. "Easy, he instructed. You're supposed to start slow."

"Did we get her?" Kelsey asked as soon as she could speak rather than croak.

Surprise flashed through Garrett's eyes. "I thought you'd want know… Your surgery… "

Kelsey waved her hand dismissively. How she felt really had nothing to do with her physical injuries. All of that would be manageable if they had put the vice president away and were free. "I uploaded information to Homeland Security from that base where we were held," Kelsey persisted. "Did it provide enough evidence on Lewis? Has she been arrested?"

Garrett hesitated.

Kelsey understood the look. He didn't want to tell her. He was worried she wouldn't be able to handle it.

"Tell me," she insisted.

"No. She has not been arrested. The information you retrieved was amazing, valuable intel on that group of mercenaries and their activities and involvement with the terrorist ring Phillip Saunders was involved in, among other crimes. Unfortunately, there was nothing to tie them to Lewis."

Alarm shot through Kelsey. "So if she's still at large, we need to get out of here! She's still going to come after us!"

Garrett placed a calming hand on her arm. "No, she won't. We're safe. The pressure on her is too much right now. Andrews let some information leak to the right people, who started asking questions about why so many resources were being used to bring in a rogue agent who'd been pulled off a case that was supposedly a dead end. That's why Lewis resorted to sending the mercenaries after us. But you took them out and stole the entirety of their mission history. There was a lot of information. Andrews still has people combing through it, but nothing has been found to link them with Vice President Lewis."

Kelsey groaned and put her hand to her head in frustration.

"Hey, don't feel bad," Garrett soothed. "We're safe, and that may not have happened if you hadn't retrieved the mercenary files. Right now, it's too risky for Lewis to come after us. It would raise too many questions. She knows we have no evidence; otherwise she would have been arrested already. We just have suspicions, and now others share those same suspicions. But that's all. It wouldn't gain anything for her to take us out.

Although, I suppose she could still arrange for a convenient accident...." Garrett mused thoughtfully.

Kelsey looked for a pillow to toss at him. "You aren't helping!" she hissed.

"Nope, nothing to worry about," Garrett assured with a wave of his hand. "Too risky. For now, she's in the clear and wants to keep it that way."

"So, the evidence we got from Phillip must have been destroyed by the mercenaries." Kelsey felt nauseated. "All of that work, and Phillip was killed over it. And now we have nothing to show for it."

Garrett nodded. "Our agents didn't find anything when they swept the building. The evidence from Rachel's scrapbook was likely destroyed immediately, and Lewis knows it."

Garrett paused and looked at Kelsey, questions brimming in his eyes. "Kelsey, they did find other things of interest when they went through the building—like mercenaries piled up in hallways, some dead, some alive and now in custody." Garrett gently took Kelsey's hand. "Kelsey what happened?"

"Apparently, I got shot," Kelsey replied dryly.

"Twice," Garrett agreed. "But you are going to be fine. You were shot once in your left shoulder and once in your right side. Neither bullet hit vital organs, but you had considerable blood loss, and of course, you lost more blood with the surgery to remove the bullets and patch you up. You will be weak for a while, but the doctors are confident you'll make a full recovery."

Kelsey nodded. "Thanks for the report, Dr. Matthews."

Garrett shrugged. "I told them I was your boyfriend. I hope you don't mind. I needed information. And your mother, blessed woman that she is, confirmed it and gave permission for them to speak to me about your condition."

"My mother!" Kelsey gasped.

"Yes, she'll be by later. She adores me already. Of course, she's thrilled that you chose such a wonderful man," he said with feigned modesty. Putting his hands behind his neck in an expression of confident relaxation, he shot her an expectant look. "Now it's your turn to give a report."

Kelsey swallowed, but didn't speak. She didn't know where to start.

After allowing the silence to lengthen almost a full minute, Garrett said casually, "Kelsey, our men found some interesting security footage. It showed a small, dark-haired woman, who kind of looks like Snow White, taking out numerous armed mercenaries in a matter of seconds. What I found most curious, though, was the woman wasn't defending anyone. She was protecting herself."

Kelsey swallowed and finally, bravely lifted her eyes to meet his. "I thought about everything you said, Garrett. Sitting there with a gun to my head, being forced to hack several different government agencies, I had to turn to the only One who could help me. And He did. I gave my life to God, and somehow, He showed me how to save it. Everything fell into place. I hacked into Homeland Security and used my own program to fool the mercenaries while I uploaded their information back up to our department. The mercenaries came back, pulled out the gun, and demanded I do more. I don't know how, but I did what I have never been able to do. I fought for myself, because I was of value to God. I took out the guys in that room, and then I fought my way out of the building."

"I'm proud of you," Garrett said softly, taking her hand back in his.

"It wasn't me," Kelsey replied, looking into his eyes with complete honesty.

"I know," Garrett said. "That's why I'm proud. You let God do what you couldn't do yourself."

"I never realized God could do that," Kelsey said softly. "Belonging to Him gave me a reason to fight and live. And it also didn't hurt to know I had someone else who valued me."

Her eyes dropped, feeling slightly embarrassed by her own confession. Ever since she had awoken, she'd had nagging thoughts that maybe, with the danger past, Garrett wouldn't feel the same as he had when they'd been captured and trapped. Though his presence and attentiveness should have been enough to convince her otherwise, the doubts persisted.

Now, however, as if feeling an irresistible magnetism, she hesitantly raised her gaze back up to his. And she couldn't deny the emotion radiating from those serious gray eyes. It was deep, intense, and seemed much more than simple caring.

Garrett cleared his throat. "I have to say I'll never forget the moment when I showed up with the cavalry to rescue you, and you stumbled out of the building covered with blood, having taken out everyone and rescued yourself."

"Well, you must not have done too shabby yourself," Kelsey said with a questioning lift of an eyebrow. "You managed to escape and enlist the help of those who had previously hunted you."

Garrett grimaced. "My story isn't nearly as impressive as yours. It turns out the ventilation system of the warehouse is connected with the building next door. I suspect all of those buildings in that row were once a large corporation of some kind. Anyway, rather by accident, I made my way to the next building, which was conveniently lax in the security department. When I made it outside and got away, I borrowed the cell phone of the first person I found and called Andrews to pick me up. Fortunately, by then, the manhunt for me was being called into question. Soon after, your information from the mercenaries showed up, which pretty much validated what I said and cleared our names because, hey, we'd just provided the U.S. government with valuable intel on a ring of criminals involved in everything from drugs to terrorism. Problem solved. Both of us are back on the good guy list, and may even get a commendation before all is said and done."

Kelsey laughed, but then grimaced with the pain. She wasn't sure if it was the pain or the intense relief of knowing they were safe and no longer on the run, but she felt tears prick the back of her eyes.

However, as great the relief was of knowing the danger was past and her job still intact, Kelsey couldn't help but feel a nagging, unsettled feeling.

They hadn't completed the mission and closed the case. The villain behind an unknown amount of evil was still walking free, able to enjoy public respect while planning her next campaign for more power.

Garrett's voice drew her back from her thoughts. "I should warn you, though," he said seriously. "Things might not be completely the same when you go back to the office. Andrews has been rather lax with his security of that hallway footage. That particular scene seems to be making the rounds of our Homeland Security department."

"Oh, great," Kelsey moaned. "That's all I need."

"Kelsey, you were unbelievable. No one has seen anything like the way you took out those mercenaries. I think you are going to have people parting like the Red Sea in front of your every move."

"What did Rachel say?" Kelsey couldn't help but ask. If the video was making the rounds, there was no question that Rachel had seen it.

Garrett's mouth quirked in a grin. "I believe her exact words were, 'That's my girl.' But you can talk to her yourself when she calls. She and Dawson have been driving me nuts with their constant need for updates. It was all Dawson could do to keep Rachel from hopping on a plane from Montana."

"Montana!" Kelsey shot up in bed, sending red hot pain shooting in two streaks across her body.

Garrett jumped up and gently pushed her back to the pillows of the bed.

Words flew rapidly from her lips. "What day is it? When is the wedding? I have to get out of here! I'm the maid of honor. I'm supposed to do the bachelorette party!"

"Calm down, Kelsey. It's—"

The door opened and a perky nurse arrived to check Kelsey's vitals, effectively postponing Kelsey's panic.

"How is your pain level?" she asked after making quick work of blood pressure and temperature tasks.

"Not too bad," Kelsey assured, ignoring the searing pain.

"Kelsey, you were shot twice. You're entitled to some pain." To the nurse, he said. "Don't listen to anything she says. She's in pain, and it's been getting worse as I've been talking to her, even though she's trying to hide it."

The nurse nodded. "I'll give you a dose now in your IV. You can have another dose if this doesn't work. Tomorrow we'll try to move you to oral medication, but you need to be eating before we do that. Oh, and this medication will probably make you very drowsy, but sleep is a good thing."

The nurse turned to Garrett and handed him the hospital menu. "Make sure she gets something to eat at some point. And call me if she needs more pain meds."

"Will do," Garrett nodded, ignoring the dirty look Kelsey shot him.

With a final assurance that the doctor would talk to Kelsey when making his rounds, the nurse exited with a click of the door.

"Rachel—" Kelsey began.

"Don't worry," Garrett said, holding up his hand to halt her words. "Rachel and Dawson are getting everything ready. You have a few days still. With any luck, you will be out of the hospital, and we will both be in Montana by Saturday."

Kelsey leaned her head back, relieved.

"Rachel did ask if you'd tried on the bridesmaid dress," Garrett said nonchalantly. "I assured her that you did and that it met with my approval."

Kelsey was not one to blush, but if she was, she would have turned quite pink at the memory of exactly how much he liked that dress. She both longed to meet Garrett's eyes and hide her head under her blankets. The thought that Garrett truly liked her, found her attractive, and wanted to be with her was all still so new. Especially since, right now, everything about the last couple of days, especially the memory of his kisses, had a hazy dreamlike quality to it.

After all that had happened, could it be possible that everything would work out? She and Garrett were safe, their jobs were still intact, and she would make it to Rachel and Dawson's wedding. After this entire mess, she might actually come out better on the other side. After all, she now had faith in God who loved her.

She opened her eyes drowsily and looked down at Garrett's warm hand clasped around hers. Could it be possible that she may also leave this nightmare with a happily ever after?

At the lovely thought, everything started to blur. She felt Garrett pull her blanket up and move her hair from her forehead in a gentle caress. Then she felt his lips lightly feather a kiss where her hair had been. She longed to tip her head up and meet his lips with hers, but her sluggish muscles wouldn't obey.

Instead, she was carried away on the wings of sleep. Yet it wasn't quite a peaceful sleep, dreaming of her happily ever after. Somehow, she couldn't shake the nagging feeling that she had left something unfinished.

It was that unshakable sense of foreboding that wouldn't let her enjoy the moment. Because for Kelsey, that final moment hadn't yet arrived. Not when, deep down, she knew the mission wasn't over.

Chapter 21

" Garrett, knock it off! Someone will see us!"

"I don't really care," he said, nuzzling up to her neck and trailing kisses from her bare shoulder to her ear. "Keeping things secret was your idea. The only thing that matters at the moment is that I finally have your attention. I called you three times, and when you didn't respond, I had to resort to other measures—ones that I'm thoroughly enjoying."

Kelsey swatted him away with her free hand and stepped back, hoping the tree they were standing behind shielded them from the eyes of the other rehearsal dinner guests crowded around the tables on the lawn of the Saunders' Montana ranch.

"You know I don't want to take attention away from Rachel and Dawson," Kelsey whispered. "This is their time. After the wedding, I have no problem letting everyone know I snagged James Bond."

Garrett wiggled his eyebrows and stepped forward with a roguish grin, as if fully prepared to reenact a James Bond kissing scene.

Kelsey held up her hand to stop him. "Stay back," she warned. "Even with one arm in a sling, I can still take you down."

"I don't doubt it," Garrett said, relaxing and leaning against the tree.

"I am sorry I didn't hear when you called me," Kelsey said. "What did you want?"

The humor in Garrett's eyes was replaced with concern. "I was just checking to see how you are doing. Are you sure you're up to going tonight? Is the pain still bad? You were totally spaced out there, which isn't like you at all."

"I'm fine. I was just preoccupied with my thoughts, I guess." She didn't really want to admit what particular thoughts were preoccupying her. Garrett might call her obsessive or tell her to just let it go. But no matter how much she wanted to, she couldn't shake the feeling that she was missing something. Yes, she didn't like the idea that they hadn't been able to get the bad guy, which in this case was a woman. But it was more than that. Her mind kept going over and over that last conversation with Phillip, analyzing each word he'd spoken, feeling like there had to be something more, if she could just figure it out.

"Oh, really?" Garrett questioned. "What kind of thoughts are you preoccupied with? Hopefully, they have something to do with the spectacularly handsome agent who's crazy about you."

Kelsey smiled. There was no half-way with Garrett. Once he decided on something, he went all in, holding nothing back. It was one of the things she liked and respected about him. It was the reason he had not given up on his assignment, even when he was ordered to do so and his life was at risk.

Because of that, she would be very surprised if Garrett was fully satisfied with their mission. Whether or not he said so, Kelsey suspected that he was bothered by it just as much as she was. But, then again, he was putting a great deal of effort on his newest all-in decision—her.

"I'll admit you are mildly distracting," Kelsey said impishly.

"Good. Then you won't mind me tagging along to mildly distract you tonight."

Kelsey laughed outright. "You can't be serious! It's a bachelorette party! No boys allowed! Besides, you're doing your own party for Dawson."

"I have everything set up for Dawson. I don't technically need to be there. Besides, I don't feel right about leaving you. You just got out of the hospital yesterday. With the late flight last night and the rehearsal today, you've got to be exhausted."

"I'm fine, Garrett," Kelsey assured, finding his attentiveness amusing. "Besides, Rachel is more than able to fill your over-protective shoes. Go have fun at your party, if you can call it that. Don't you think you could have come up with a better party than just going target practicing?"

"And you did so much better at planning Rachel's party?" Garrett said, raising his eyebrows and folding his arms across his chest expectantly.

"Yes, I did," Kelsey said proudly. "I reserved a hotel suite in Helena. We're having a combination bachelorette party and bridal shower. I even have games planned. Then we'll watch movies and eat a bunch of junk food."

Garrett snorted. "Where did you get all those ideas? Pinterest? Rachel would have liked target practicing just as much."

Kelsey made a playful swipe at Garrett with her good hand. He danced out of the way with a grin.

Kelsey would never admit it, but Garrett was actually right. She had considered target practicing for her party agenda, but with time on her hands in the hospital, she had indulged in Pinterest and found some great ideas. Now she just hoped Rachel liked the party and her plans didn't end up in the category of Pinterest flops!

"Matthews, you ready to go?" Dawson called, walking toward them from where the tables were emptying of the final guests remaining from the rehearsal dinner.

"I don't feel right about leaving you." Garrett said again, his brow worried.

"Go." Kelsey said firmly. "Rachel and I will be leaving soon as well. You've been babysitting me all week. I promise to behave. Go have fun."

Garrett shot her one more worried look, and Kelsey could tell he wanted to kiss her goodbye.

"No," Kelsey whispered, glancing nervously at Dawson, who had stopped to talk to someone only a few feet away.

"Fine," Garrett said stiffly. "But as soon as this wedding is over, you'd better make it up to me." Clicking his heels together at attention, he gave a brisk, formal salute to Kelsey, then he turned to meet Dawson.

Kelsey laughed at his choice of goodbye, while Dawson shot confused looks back and forth between them.

The two men soon disappeared around the front of the house. Feeling suddenly weak, Kelsey leaned back against the tree, letting the trunk support her weight. Despite her bravado with Garrett, she was tired, and judging from her pain level, it was time for her medication.

She sighed and looked around. The white-clad tables shone elegantly in the Montana sun. The wedding rehearsal had gone well, and afterward, the tables had been well-staffed with guests for the outdoor dinner. Tomorrow, the Saunders' large backyard would be even more lavishly decorated for the wedding, with the tables restocked for the reception following the ceremony.

A few guests still lingered this evening, with a glowing Rachel still center stage visiting with her well-wishers. Kelsey could go back and sit at one of the tables, but she didn't want to risk someone trying to converse with her. She didn't feel like talking, and she also didn't feel like fending off questions as to why her arm was in a sling.

Instead, she turned her gaze to the house and let her thoughts return to their familiar pattern.

It didn't make sense. Phillip was not the type to put all of his eggs in one basket, so to speak. He was too smart for that. If he had gone to so much trouble to acquire and preserve all of the evidence Kelsey had found in Rachel's album, wouldn't he also have a backup of some kind? In Kelsey's mind, there was no way he would have risked only one cache of evidence. So if that was true, what did he do with the backup?

Deep in thought, her mind replayed that last conversation with Phillip. An idea slowly formed. Her eyes sharpened, and she looked at the scene in front of her. The sun was setting, sending a gradient of color across the sky, while below, Rachel's parents' house sat silently.

Kelsey suddenly left the tree and walked forward. She went through the back door of the house and stopped. Everyone was outside, and now, completely focused on her task, Kelsey lost herself in thought. Though her body didn't move a muscle, her mind roved through the house. Then, almost as if in a state of trance-like focus, she walked to Rachel's bedroom.

Kelsey was staying in a guest room down the hall, but it was Rachel's room that held her attention.

She paused in the doorway.

"But if I could, I'd go back to the beginning. I wouldn't let Rachel go on that stupid trip to New York. I'd hide her infernal suitcase that started this whole mess and undo everything from the last year and a half. I'd hand in evidence the first time I was approached and take up ranching like I always should have!"

Phillip's words echoed through her mind as clearly as if he'd just spoken them. He said he wished he could go back to the beginning. He wanted to redo everything. No New York trip. No suitcase.

The suitcase.

But that was impossible. Rachel's suitcase had been destroyed in New York when Rachel and Dawson had thrown it and the bomb it contained out of the helicopter. It had exploded in one fantastic blast off the shore of New York. Kelsey herself had purchased Rachel a new suitcase to take home to Montana, but it had looked nothing like that original one that had started it all.

Thoughtfully, Kelsey walked forward and opened Rachel's closet door. There, nestled in the corner, beneath a few clothes Rachel had left hanging, was a red suitcase. An exact replica of the original she had taken to New York.

Kelsey pulled the suitcase out and unzipped it. It was completely empty. In fact, it looked as if it had never been used. Kelsey searched every pocket and crease, but found nothing.

Finally, she stuck her hand in a small side pocket and ran in along the length. She almost didn't feel it. But her fingernail caught on a thread in the corner, and she stopped.

Wiggling her fingers back into the corner, she felt a small, square bulge. It was so small and unnoticeable, it would have gone undetected by anyone not specifically looking for it.

Kelsey usually carried a pocketknife, but since she'd worn a sundress for the rehearsal, she had needed to forgo her gun and pocketknife that accessorized her usual attire. She had managed to stick her cell phone in a tiny pocket hidden in flounces of her skirt, but that was it. Although a gun and a knife weren't considered necessary items for a wedding rehearsal, Kelsey would have liked to have found a way to carry them anyway—strapped to her leg if necessary. But her shoulder and its accompanying sling her arm made her usual measures practically impossible, forcing her to forgo her normal and rely on Garrett and her other agent friends, who would likely carry their "just-in-case supplies" even if meeting the pope!

Jumping up, she went to Rachel's desk and began searching through the drawers. Finding a pair of scissors, she went back to the suitcase and struggled to use the scissors without adequate assistance from her arm in the sling. Finally succeeding in cutting out the small bulge, she lifted it up and extracted from the fabric a small memory card.

Kelsey quickly stood and turned to the computer on Rachel's desk. It booted up quickly. She slid the card into the reader and waited, tapping her foot while the contents downloaded.

Completed, she clicked on the file. Her heart leapt. It was a digital copy of every bit of evidence she had found in Rachel's album.

Over the past few days, Kelsey had given considerable thought to what she could have done differently with Phillip's evidence. Now, she didn't ask advice or permission. Without a second of hesitation, she put those regrets to the work of redemption.

Kelsey impatiently chewed her lower lip. Kelsey lost track on how long she sat there. Unfortunately, it was a large file and manipulating it multiple places was taking longer than she'd like. She drummed her fingers on the desk, idly watching the little green bars creep across the screen.

"Agent Johnson, I want to commend you on a job well done."

Kelsey swung around right as the computer screen shattered with two well-placed bullets.

Standing in the doorway to Rachel's room was the vice president of the United States, with gun in hand.

Victoria Lewis sighed. "This is all so tiresome. I really wanted to let you live. Unfortunately, I suspected my dear Phillip had another copy of his documents, and I thought it was likely here in Montana. We've destroyed everything else remotely connected to him, even an automated email full of gibberish and set to send to his sister upon his death. So we've been watching, waiting, figuring that you would eventually lead us right to it. And since I knew I'd need to be around to make sure no one messed up this time, I made a convenient visit to the quaint state of Montana."

Lewis was flanked by at least three armed men.

"Holmes?" Kelsey's voice croaked, recognizing the suited man to Lewis's right.

"Oh, yes," Lewis smiled. "Agent Holmes has been very helpful. He's destined for great things. Now, Holmes, if you would kindly check the computer, we can get on with the business at hand."

Kelsey looked at her fellow agent in disgust as Holmes walked to the computer and removed the memory chip. He was a mediocre agent who took care of logistics associated with Homeland Security.

He frequently assisted Andrews and had never been tasked as a field agent. His association with Lewis explained a lot about how Kelsey and Garrett had been so easily tracked. Holmes must have been providing any intel that came through Homeland Security, and Andrews specifically.

Without any ceremony, Holmes took out the chip, smashed it with the butt of his gun and tossed it into a glass of water sitting on Rachel's desk.

"Now, the question is what to do with you," Lewis mused. "Should we kill her here or take her with us? If we take her, there is a greater chance of being seen."

A wave of helplessness washed over Kelsey. She didn't see a way out. She was unarmed, with her left shoulder and arm completely immobilized, and since Holmes had returned to stand with the others, she was about 8 feet away from the nearest attacker. She was outgunned and out-numbered against people who fully intended to kill her. And with the silencers on their weapons, they could accomplish the deed with no one the wiser.

Is this it? She silently asked God.

Somehow, that didn't seem so scary. She had done everything she could, and if they killed her, she would have the satisfaction of knowing she had done what was needed.

"Kelsey, are you in here?" A voice called with the slamming of the back door.

Kelsey's momentary peace was shattered with terror.

Rachel!

With a brief nod from Lewis, the three men got into position. The instant they had a line of sight on Rachel, she would be killed.

She remembered Phillip's last request. He had wanted Kelsey to protect his family at all costs. And Kelsey had promised.

Kelsey inhaled slowly. If it cost her everything, she would keep that promise. They would not hurt Rachel.

Without forming a plan, Kelsey reached down, picked up the suitcase at her feet, and flung it at the vice president.

Pain seared like fire in Kelsey's shoulder, but before the suitcase even found its mark, she was running across the room.

The suitcase hit Lewis in the head.

Startled, the men turned toward her shriek.

Kelsey jumped, snapping a kick in Holmes' face, knocking him back into one of the other men. The third man swung his gun around and fired right as Kelsey knocked the barrel up with her good arm. The shot hit the ceiling.

Kelsey landed a groin kick and grabbed for the weapon, but with only one hand, her fingers slipped, and the gun knocked to the floor.

She heard the other men behind her.

"Rachel!" she shrieked.

With a rapid succession of thumps, Kelsey knew the moment Rachel joined the fight. Knowing her friend could handle herself, Kelsey focused on the man in front of her. With a crescent kick to the head, he was down. Kelsey snatched up the gun off the floor and turned.

Simultaneously, she saw Victoria Lewis flee out the door, while Holmes, on the ground a few feet from Rachel, lifted his head and raised his gun.

Rachel, having already disposed of one attacker, was fighting a fourth man who must have been stationed somewhere as a guard. With Rachel's back turned, Kelsey knew her friend didn't see the weapon aimed her direction

As if in slow motion, Kelsey saw Holmes take aim, positioning his finger on the trigger.

Without hesitation, Kelsey shot the gun in her hand. A single bullet, and Holmes' gun fell lifelessly on the floor.

Rachel kicked, grabbed the gun from the final assailant, and dropped him with a swift hand strike to the neck.

"Go after her!" she shouted to Kelsey, even as one of the men on the floor dared to raise his head. "I've got this!"

Kelsey took off. She ran through the house and out the front door, the screen door slamming behind her. Up ahead, she saw Lewis, head down and walking rapidly through the cars, lining the road, trying not to attract attention. It looked as if she was on her way to a cluster of vehicles parked beneath a tree.

Kelsey ran, but the sling confined her movement and slowed her down. Reaching over with her good hand, she ripped the sling off and threw it down. Now pumping both arms, she ignored the pain and started gaining on the vice president.

Lewis turned around, saw Kelsey, and took off running. She was surprisingly quick and made it to the cars. She flung open the car door, right as Kelsey caught up to her.

Kelsey grabbed for Lewis's perfectly styled blonde hair, yanking her back away from the car.

Lewis shrieked, but twisted around and grabbed at Kelsey's left shoulder. Excruciating pain shot through Kelsey's entire body. Her grip lessened, and suddenly, Lewis had a gun planed in Kelsey's chest.

Though the older woman still held a tight squeeze on her shoulder with one hand, Kelsey gritted her teeth, grabbed her gun hand and twisted with every bit of strength she had left.

Lewis shrieked, Kelsey felt the snap of bone, and the gun released.

With strength leaving her body, Kelsey dropped low, barely managing to lift her leg in a heel kick to the back of Lewis's knee. Lewis dropped to the ground.

The gun now in her hand, Kelsey dragged herself up on shaking feet.

Lewis was pulling herself up as well.

Stumbling forward, Kelsey lifted her foot and snapped a fumbling kick to the chest, knocking her flat on her back. With fingers trembling in weakness, Kelsey lifted the gun, pointing it down at Victoria Lewis.

"Careful," Lewis warned. "Do you really want to shoot the vice president of the United States? Nobody will believe you. The best scenario is that you get out of here alive, after assaulting me and my security team." She sneered. "All your 'evidence' has been destroyed. You have nothing on me."

"You're wrong," Kelsey said breathlessly. "It's over. You're over. You destroyed the memory card, but it's a lot more difficult to destroy something that's been uploaded to the cloud."

Lewis's eyes widened.

"Yes," Kelsey assured. "I copied everything from that card onto a drive in the cloud. Now there's nowhere you can go to destroy it. It also helps that it's a rather public drive. At least, pretty much everyone in Homeland Security has access to it, so it wouldn't do any good to take me out."

Complete horror wreathed Lewis's pale face.

And Kelsey continued casually, "Oh, did I also mention that the files also uploaded to every major news network, government agency, and social media network? Now I don't know that all of those finished uploading before you shot the computer," Kelsey mused thoughtfully. "But some of the little green lines managed to get to the end."

Fighting nausea, Kelsey held the gun steady with her good hand, and fighting the pain, she reached into the pocket of her sundress with the other one. "If you'll excuse me, I just have to check my phone." She pushed the button, bringing the phone to life. "Oh, good. One of my photos posted to Facebook. It was a particularly juicy one. And look, it's already getting some 'likes!'"

"But... I didn't... Nobody... "

Somehow, it was quite satisfying to see the articulate woman reduced to stuttering.

"If you're wondering why you didn't receive some kind of warning from one of your informants, that's because you couldn't. I was not under orders. I did not ask permission. I distributed the information as far and as wide as I could. And it's amazing how far and wide you can go in about five minutes."

Rage and hate twisted Lewis features into almost a caricature of her political façade. She raised herself up as if attempting to stand.

"I wouldn't do that," Kelsey said, her tone deceptively relaxed. "To answer your original question: no. I don't have a problem shooting the vice president of the United States. However, you can rest assured that I won't kill you. There are plenty of places I can shoot that won't kill you, but will hurt an awful lot. You see, I want you alive to face trial and be convicted of your crimes. I want you to feel the derision of the entire country. And then, I want you to spend the rest of your life in a maximum security prison. But if you want to try to get up, I can shoot you a couple of times. I've heard the knee is quite painful, though I can speak about the shoulder from personal experience. So which one would you prefer to start with?"

Lewis froze, though Kelsey feared it was only momentary. The emotion on Lewis's face was rapidly changing from anger to desperation. Someone desperate was foolish and dangerous.

But Kelsey had no idea what to do. She glanced down at her phone, still trying to keep her focus on Lewis. But the screen was blurring, and her hands shaking so badly that she didn't think she could manage to call anyone. Besides, she didn't think they could make it in time. She knew she was bleeding and was pretty sure her wounds had reopened. She was already so weak that she was nauseated and seeing spots in her vision.

She didn't think she could make it back to the Saunders house by herself, let alone prod Lewis along and make sure she didn't try anything. She had no handcuffs or rope to secure her captive, just a gun that was becoming increasingly heavy to hold in position.

Kelsey looked up, trying to gauge the distance to the house and her chances of making it. She saw Rachel come out the front door and start running toward her.

But the black spots were becoming larger in Kelsey's vision, and it felt as if a vise was slowly restricting her breathing.

Rachel wouldn't make it in time.

Just then, a car braked hard, stopping on the road right beside them. Kelsey saw two figures jump out of the car, heard the slamming of the car doors. For the briefest of instants, her eyes cleared enough for her to recognize Garrett, now just a few yards away.

The wave of relief was so intense that it seemed to leach all of the air from Kelsey's body and the strength from each muscle. The black dots shut off all light, and Kelsey felt herself falling. But somehow, she never reached the ground.

For the first time in her life, Kelsey Johnson fainted.

Chapter 22

Kelsey watched anxiously as Dawson fed Rachel the wedding cake, careful not to smear any on his new wife's face.

Thank goodness Rachel had married a smart man.

Rachel had let it be known that if her new husband dared to smash the cake in her face, then he would quickly find himself flat on his back.

With the ceremony, the toasts, and now the cake all marked as complete, Kelsey sighed in relief. She had made it.

"Are you okay?" Garrett asked, holding tightly to her arm.

Realizing she must have leaned too heavily on him for support, Kelsey quickly assured, "I'm fine. Just relieved that I made it through the wedding."

"Let's find you a seat at a table. For someone who shouldn't be out of the hospital, you've held up extremely well."

Kelsey shot a glance at Rachel, making sure her maid of honor duties weren't needed, and then consented to let Garrett lead her to a table.

"I'll go get you some cake and something to drink," Garrett said, but then he looked back at her uncertainly.

"Go," Kelsey ordered. "I'll behave."

"I've heard that before," Garrett grumbled. "Then you went and took out an army of bad guys and the vice president."

Kelsey just smiled serenely.

Giving up, Garrett walked away, still shooting cautious glances back at her every few seconds.

Kelsey turned back to watch Rachel. Her friend made a beautiful bride. The off-the-shoulder wedding dress was simple, yet beautiful for an outdoor wedding. The weather was gorgeous—the Spring air not yet too hot, but with a bright sun lighting a big, blue Montana sky and making Rachel's long, loose, blonde hair shine like gold.

Kelsey's favorite part of the entire ceremony was watching her friend's face. Her smile was one of complete joy, and with the way she looked at

Dawson, you couldn't help but know that this was meant to be.

Of course, with everything that happened last night, there had been talk of postponing the wedding, but Kelsey was so glad they had decided to go ahead. For her part, Kelsey had outright defied the doctor's orders, insisting on leaving the hospital after they had sewn her back up. In Kelsey's mind, the greatest casualties of the night were Rachel and Dawson's parties.

It was only after she'd left the hospital that she'd learned Rachel and Dawson's accounts of the night.

While on their way to the shooting range, Garrett had idly checked Facebook when Dawson stopped for gas. Seeing Kelsey's post, he and Dawson had turned around and were already tearing back to the Saunders' ranch when Rachel called, frantically telling them what had happened. But by then, they were almost there.

Rachel had enlisted her dad's help to watch the prisoners, and had run out of the house looking for Kelsey and Lewis. But Garrett and Dawson got there first. Rachel had looked up to see Garrett barely manage to catch Kelsey before she hit the ground.

Rachel called for an ambulance, and then for a Homeland Security clean-up crew and everything else involved in arresting the Vice President of the United States. By the time all of the reporting and logistics were handed over to trusted superiors and put to rest for the night, Rachel and Dawson's parties were long over.

Kelsey had heard Rachel and Dawson's accounts of what had happened, and felt bad that their special nights had been ruined. But now, after watching the beautiful ceremony, Kelsey realized that it really didn't matter. Rachel and Dawson had gotten their happy ending anyway.

Kelsey smiled her thanks when Garrett returned with cake and punch. They ate slowly while watching Rachel dance with her dad. Kelsey glanced over at Rachel's mom and was pleased to see that both of Rachel's parents seemed more at peace today than they had since Phillip had been arrested.

After returning late from the hospital last night, Kelsey had insisted on telling them her entire conversation with Phillip. She insisted that if not for Phillip's evidence, Victoria Lewis would have never been apprehended.

Kelsey had also related how Phillip was concerned for their safety, asking Kelsey to protect them. Finally, and perhaps most importantly, Kelsey was able to relate Phillip's words about God, giving the grieving parents hope that maybe their son had made things right with the Lord before he'd died.

Kelsey momentarily let her mind drift back to last night, and once again, she saw Carson Saunders' face after she had finished her report. When the depth of Phillip's crimes had been discovered, it had devastated his father. After learning of those last few minutes of his life, tears streamed down the big man's face, and a spark lit his eyes. While his wife sobbed, completely overcome with emotion, Mr. Saunders had wrapped his arms around Kelsey and whispered a broken, 'thank you.' Kelsey had the distinct impression that by telling of Phillip's final actions, she had given Carson Saunders back his son.

It was a special moment for Kelsey, just as it was special now to see Rachel dance with her father at her wedding.

The wedding ceremony itself had been just about perfect, and there was an added peace and joy in everything, knowing that the case that had haunted them all for so long was finally laid to rest, and the persons responsible brought to justice. Kelsey knew that the closure and hope the older couple had been given last night allowed them a greater capacity for joy in their daughter's wedding. And Kelsey felt blessed to have been a part of it.

Kelsey knew that underneath it all, Rachel was still having a hard time with Phillip's death. Though she had heard his entire last conversation herself and shared the same relief and hope as her parents, Rachel still carried a shadow of grief around her eyes that never disappeared, no matter how happy her friend seemed. The family was planning a small, private memorial for Phillip, after his body was released following the ongoing investigation. The family had felt the best, most healing route, was for Rachel and Dawson to go forward with their plans for the wedding. And seeing all of their faces now, Kelsey was very thankful that they had.

Dawson soon stepped into his father-in-law's place as Rachel's dance partner. Carson kissed his daughter's cheek and placed her hand into Dawson's.

Kelsey watched the newlyweds dance, feeling such happiness for her friends.

"You feel up to dancing?" Garrett said beside her.

Kelsey smiled up at Garrett. "Of course. I should put those dance classes to some use."

Garrett pulled Kelsey out to where other couples were joining Rachel and Dawson. Unfortunately, Kelsey was much weaker than she liked to admit, and depended on Garrett for support way too much, but he didn't seem to mind.

Garrett held her close, and Kelsey was glad for both his support of her weight and for his intoxicating nearness.

"You scared me to death yesterday," Garrett whispered in her ear. "But at the same time, I'm so proud of you. I don't know anyone, man or woman, who could have fought like you did, with two bullet wounds. The pain must have been incredible, and yet, you took out armed men and single-handedly apprehended the vice president."

"I had Rachel's help with the security team," Kelsey said modestly. "And I was rather motivated to not let that evil woman escape."

Garrett shook his head. "From what Rachel said, you saved her life."

"I had a promise to keep," Kelsey answered. "And, thank the Lord, He gave me the strength to do so."

Garrett smiled. "And you just gave me another reason to be proud of you. Yes, I'm also very thankful that He kept you safe for me. He must have been listening to my frantic prayers. After I saw that Facebook post, I didn't know if I would make it. Dawson must have seen how upset I was.

He wouldn't let me drive. However, he himself was considerably less agitated after Rachel called."

"Have you heard from Andrews at all?" Kelsey said worriedly. "I kind of expected him to call and lecture me on my method of evidence distribution. I didn't obtain permission, I just distributed it as much as I could, thinking that might be the only way to keep Lewis and her wide network from choking it out. But I know the media is having a field day, every government agency is scrambling, and the president and every other politician is attempting intense damage control."

Garrett threw his head back and laughed. "Kelsey, Andrews wants to nominate you for any award he can and get a few buildings named after you as well. Fortunately, his better sense has made him work hard to keep your name out of all reports, which hasn't been easy. Everyone wants to know the name of the agent who cracked the biggest case of the century and brought the Vice President of the United States to justice, and in such a spectacular way as to post all the evidence to every news and social media site."

"I worried about that," Kelsey said honestly. "My name may have been attached as the sender in some of the emails and posts. I didn't have a chance to hide my identity very well."

Garrett nodded. "All your files are classified at the highest level. 'Kelsey Johnson is a fairly common name. If worst comes to worst, Andrews will refer to you as Agent Johnson, but stipulate that the nature of your work requires anonymity. Right now, no one even knows you're a woman."

"So you talked to Andews?"

"Yes, he called immediately after we got to the hospital last night. He was concerned about you, wanting to make sure you were okay. He thought what you did was brilliant. The only person he was berating was himself. He's angry with himself for not realizing that Holmes was an informant for Lewis, and now he's actively sorting through evidence to identify any other associates. All government agencies are in a panic. More high level people are being arrested based on the evidence you retrieved. Kelsey, the entire country should be in your debt, and Andrews knows it. Unfortunately, I think he'll want to put you into field work now, and I don't like that idea at all."

Kelsey grimaced. "I don't know that I like that idea either. After so many years of feeling inferior because field work was the one thing I wasn't qualified to do, now I think I could really do without it. After two bullets and enough adrenaline to last a lifetime, I think the whole idea is entirely over-rated. Send me back to my desk, computer, and nice, neat facts."

The music changed and a faster-paced song replaced the slower, romantic one. Knowing she wouldn't be able to keep up, Kelsey broke from Garrett and took his hand to return to their table.

But as they passed a hedge of lilac bushes in bloom with bunches of fragrant purple flowers, Kelsey suddenly felt her feet swept out from under her as Garrett kidnapped her to the other side.

"You know I like that dress," he whispered, his breath warm against her cheek. "Dawson and Rachel are married. Do I have the all-clear to show the woman I love how beautiful and wonderful I think she is, or should we keep things just for a romantic rendezvous behind the bushes?"

Kelsey blinked up at Garrett, fumbling for words. What had he just said?

"Yes, you heard me right," Garrett said seriously, his eyes losing all trace of teasing. He paused, gently caressing her face, as if wiping away all trace of confusion. "Kelsey, we've known each other for years. I don't want you to think I'm speaking from the adrenaline of the last week, because I'm not. The truth is, I've been in love with you for most, if not all of the years I've known you, but I fought hard against it."

Momentarily, he broke eye contact, as if struggling to put his emotions into words. Then, resolutely he raised his eyes to meet hers once more and continued. "Feeling something so deep for someone scared me to death. But everything that has happened has shown me a greater fear. Kelsey, I can't lose you. Maybe all the adrenaline opened my heart to realize how much I feel for you, and now that we share the same faith, there is nothing to hold us back."

The vulnerability in his gray eyes took her breath away.

He gently raised her hands to his lips, keeping her eyes locked with his. "Kelsey, I madly, deeply love you. I was an idiot to fight so hard against someone who is the best thing that could ever happen to me. In our line of work, we have no guarantee of tomorrow, and yet, now I know that what I want most is to spend all of my tomorrows with you."

Kelsey's breath caught in a sob right before Garrett's lips claimed hers.

"I love you too, Garrett," she whispered between kisses. "I always have."

With her weight entirely supported in Garrett's arms, she barely noticed when her feet once again left the ground. She wrapped her good arm around Garrett's neck, running her fingers through his hair as he cradled her close, continuing to thoroughly kiss her.

"Agent Johnson! Agent Matthews!" A loud voice called, as if right on the other side of the bushes. "Report for duty!"

Garrett's mouth ripped from Kelsey's, and he barely managed not to drop her. Her feet met the ground, and Kelsey attempted to fix her mussed hair while hurrying around the hedge. She glanced at Garrett, hoping he didn't have her lipstick all over his lips.

She saw him swiftly wipe his mouth and hoped that would be enough.

"There you are!" Dawson exclaimed as they came into sight.

"We're ready to do the bouquet and garter toss!" Rachel said brightly.

Garrett slapped Dawson on the back. "Let's hurry and get you two off on your honeymoon."

"You're reading my mind," Dawson said, raising an eyebrow to Rachel.

Rachel blushed crimson to the point that her coloring reminded Kelsey of something. "I don't suppose you packed a certain red suitcase for your honeymoon?" she asked teasingly.

Rachel grimaced. "Absolutely not! That thing showed up in my closet soon after New York. I assumed my mom had gotten it for me, trying to be nice by replacing the original. But I never mentioned it to her because I didn't want to hurt her feelings by telling her I couldn't stand the sight of the thing. Now I know that it was Phillip who put it there, but I still have no idea how you figured it out, Kelsey."

"It wasn't easy," Kelsey admitted. "You heard the very cryptic things Phillip said to me. But I kept going back to how he said he wished he could go back to the beginning and redo things. I realized the beginning had to be something to do with you, but I didn't know for sure what it was until I saw that red suitcase."

A sudden pain shot through Kelsey's shoulder, causing her to jerk involuntarily. She felt Garrett's arm come around her waist to support her. She flashed a smile up at him, saying, "I'm fine. It's just almost time for my meds."

"Speaking of the time," Dawson said, looking pointedly at his watch. "We have some nice *black* suitcases all packed and ready for our honeymoon, and a man who is rather anxious to have some time alone with his wife." He turned pointedly to Rachel.

Had Rachel noticed, her blush would have made an immediate return, but she was too busy looking from Garrett to Kelsey and back again. Kelsey could read the look on her face, and alarmed, followed Rachel's gaze up to Garrett, and a slight smudge of red lipstick at the corner of his mouth.

Kelsey's gaze swung back to Rachel, but it was too late.

Her friend turned to her husband, an ornery, knowing smile on her face. "So, husband," she said casually, taking Dawson's hand in hers. "I have a theoretical question. What do you think happens when James Bond and Snow White get together?"

Clearly understanding, Dawson turned an overly-innocent expression to Garrett and Kelsey. "Well, obviously, they were meant to be together. They get married and have a bunch of secret agent princesses."

"Who sing catch ballads while they fight bad guys," Rachel nodded seriously.

Dawson agreed. "And when they get in a really tight spot, woodland animals come to their rescue."

Rachel, eyes sparkling, continued. "Yes, and—"

"Nice boots, Rachel!" Kelsey flung out, much too loudly.

Rachel's words died on her lips, and her face immediately turned a brighter red than before.

Everyone's eyes immediately shot to the shoes peeking from under Rachel's wedding dress.

Dawson reached down and lifted her skirt slightly, revealing a very familiar pair of tall, black boots. "Are those…?"

Dawson suddenly lifted Rachel off her feet and carried her over to sit on a table. "If I may have your garter, Montana?" he said politely.

With face still blazing, Rachel lifted her gown so Dawson could slip off the fancy blue and white garter.

Dawson immediately tossed the garter at Garrett, who automatically caught it, a startled expression on his face.

Dawson then turned and held out his hand to help Rachel off the table.

"If you will excuse me," Rachel said politely, "I believe my husband would like to leave now. Kelsey, would you please take care of this for me?"

With a mischievous smile, Rachel tossed the bouquet directly at Kelsey, who couldn't help but catch it.

Rachel turned and marched her boots across the lawn with her husband, while the laughing guests, realizing the newlyweds were making their exit, scrambled to throw birdseed and rose petals at the rapidly departing couple.

Garrett laughed. "Boots?" he questioned Kelsey, as they followed Rachel and Dawson across the yard.

Kelsey's laughter joined Garrett's. "Those were the boots Dawson made Rachel wear when they met in New York. They needed disguises. Let's just say, the boots were the only thing Rachel deemed appropriate for saving."

"And I take it, you knew she was wearing the boots and that they would be significant to Dawson?"

"Of course. Fastest way to get Rachel to stop teasing. Mission accomplished."

Everyone was now filtering around to the front of the house where Rachel and Dawson's getaway vehicle was waiting, appropriately decked out with cans, steamers, and a hard-to-miss "Just Married" sign.

"I think we deserved Rachel's teasing and more," Garrett admitted, eyes sparkling.

Kelsey nodded. "It would seem so," Kelsey admitted, now noticing the other bright, curious looks she and Garrett were getting from friends, coworkers, and even Rachel's parents. Apparently the only people they had been fooling about their relationship was themselves.

"Dawson isn't an idiot," Garrett said. "He saw how I reacted yesterday when you were in danger. And Rachel is too smart not to notice the way I look at you." Looking around, Garrett grumbled, "And it appears that Rachel wasn't the only one with keen eyesight."

"Rachel always knows stuff," Kelsey said, slightly exasperated that their secret was apparently never a secret. "She seemed to know that I'd made my peace with God before I even told her. She was thrilled, of course. But now that I think about it, she's been looking at me with those knowing eyes and dropping hints about you. I guess I was just too distracted to notice and fess up."

Garrett wrapped his arms around Kelsey. "So now we're free," he said, placing a gentle kiss in her hair. "Free of the case that has plagued us. You're free of your past and the scars that kept you from God. And now we're free to love each other and make our future together."

Garrett suddenly released her, stepping aside as Dawson and Rachel were pelted heavily before making their getaway.

Kelsey stood on her tiptoes to watch the couple hug their parents goodbye and wave before disappearing into the red corvette that would take them away to their honeymoon.

"Yes, you're right," Kelsey mused thoughtfully, finally responding. "I guess it's kind of over. The case is closed. The bad guys caught. Rachel and Dawson are married…"

The newlyweds pulled away. Even though she doubted her friends could see, Kelsey lifted her hand and waved goodbye, watching as their car disappeared behind the trees lining the road.

With her heart full and happy, Kelsey turned to Garrett.

But he wasn't standing beside her. He was kneeling. On one knee.

And in his hands, he had a ring.

Other books by Amanda Tru

<u>YESTERDAY series:</u>
Yesterday
The Locket
Today
The Choice
Tomorrow
The Promise
Forever (coming soon)

<u>TRU EXCEPTIONS series:</u>
Baggage Claim
Mirage
Point of Origin
Rogue

<u>BRIDES BY MAIL Series:</u>
(Written with Cami Wesley)
Bride of Pretense
Bride by Request
Bride of Regret *(coming soon)*

Christian Romance:
Secret Santa
The Random Acts of Cupid
The Assumption of Guilt
The Christmas Card

Clean Romance:
The Romance of the Sugar Plum Fairy

Children's:
Under the pen name J. Lasterday
DOG THE DRAGON series:
The Dragon's Escape

About the Author

Amanda loves to write exciting books with plenty of unexpected twists. She figures she loses so much sleep writing the things, it's only fair she makes readers lose sleep with books they can't put down!

Amanda has always loved reading, and writing books has been a lifelong dream. A vivid imagination helps her write captivating stories in a wide variety of genres. Her current book list includes everything from holiday romances, to action-packed suspense, to a Christian time travel / romance series.

Amanda is a former elementary school teacher who now spends her days being mommy to three little boys and her nights furiously writing. Amanda and her family live in a small Idaho town where the number of cows outnumbers the number of people.

Connect with Amanda Tru

Amanda loves to hear from readers!

Website:
http://amandatru.com

Email:
truamanda@gmail.com

Facebook:
https://www.facebook.com/amandatru.author

Twitter:
https://twitter.com/TruAmanda

Email Sign up:
(sign up to be notified of new releases)
http://eepurl.com/ZQdw9

Please enjoy the following Sneak Peek of

Yesterday

Time Travel Romance / Christian Romantic Suspense

Chapter 1

Red flashed against the bright white of the snow.

I slammed on the brakes. The SUV skidded toward the guardrail.

My heart seemed to stop. I couldn't breathe. My body felt suspended as the mountainous terrain whirled across my vision. I braced for impact. Unexpectedly, the vehicle lurched as the tires found traction and came to a sudden stop

I sucked in air. My eyes frantically searched the heavy snowfall.

What had I seen?

Was it human?

Had I hit something?

The Sierra mountains were shrouded in the stillness of the winter storm, silent and revealing no secrets. Had I just imagined something dart in front of me?

I caught a glimpse of a fist out of the corner of my eye. I jumped. A strangled scream escaped my throat as the fist started hammering on my window. Heart thumping, I peered beyond the relentless pounding to see the outline of a woman in a red parka. She was screaming, but I couldn't understand her words.

Fingers fumbling and shaking, I rolled down my window. At her appearance, an electric current of shock ripped through me.

Blood streamed from somewhere on her head. It trickled down to her chin, leaving a dark red trail. Dirty tears streaked her cheeks, and her hair hung in clumps of frizzy knots.

I frantically jerked open my door.

"Are you okay?" I asked.

But she didn't answer. Instead, she continued to scream, her hysterical cries now slicing through me.

"Help! Help! Please help me! I can't get them out!"

What was she talking about? My eyes traced an invisible line to where she was gesturing. A few yards in front of my own fender, the meager guardrail was bent and scraped. Peering through the falling snow, I could see beyond that to where the frozen earth had been torn up. Standing on the frame of my car door, I looked into the embankment off the side. Red tail lights glowed like beacons.

The shock to my senses was like a physical blow. I sprang out of the car, stepping into a blood stained patch of snow. Blood had dripped from the woman's leg where her torn pants exposed a jagged wound. Her sobbing and frantic cries continued, but she wasn't making sense.

Her skin was chalky green. She was in shock, yet I felt paralyzed. My medical background consisted of a three hour CPR and first aid class I'd taken over a year ago. Panic washed over me like a wave. I didn't know how to help her!

Desperate, I gently pushed her toward the back seat of the SUV. Her feet shuffled forward two steps, and then she collapsed. I caught her around the shoulders and practically dragged her rag doll frame to the back seat.

She roused enough to help as I lifted her into the back seat. I unraveled the scarf from my neck and wrapped it around her leg above the bloody gash, tying it as tightly as I could.

Reaching into the back of the SUV, I located a large flashlight and my old coat that I used when skiing. I wrapped the arms of the coat loosely around her leg, hoping the bulky material would soak up some of the blood.

"What's your name?" I asked the woman.

She cleared her throat and shook her head, her brow creasing with confusion. Instead, she began a new litany of faint but frantic cries about her family.

"You can tell me later. I'm Hannah."

"Help! My family… !"

"I'm going down into the ravine right now. Stay here. I'll help them. I promise."

Hoping I didn't just make a promise I couldn't keep, I shut the door and tripped my way through the snowdrifts toward the red haloed taillights.

I pulled my phone out of my coat pocket. There usually wasn't cell phone coverage on this road. But, just maybe…

No service.

This wasn't supposed to be happening! I should be at my sister's lodge at the top of the mountain not crawling down a steep embankment to help accident victims!

It wasn't even supposed to be snowing! I'd checked the weather report at least a dozen times: no new snow for the next week. Now it was practically a blizzard!

I took deep breaths, trying to control the panic and adrenaline running through my veins as I half climbed, half slid down the incline. This wasn't me. I'm not the brave sort. In fact, I'm pretty much a wimp!

I was facing the risk of a serious panic attack even before any of this had happened. The rational part of my brain said my fear was ridiculous. The roads were supposed to be clear. I'd driven to Silver Springs many times before. And, I was driving the biggest, meanest, previously-owned SUV an over-protective father could buy for his college-age daughter. Despite my best rationale, my hands were sweating, my heart was beating erratically, and I was still at the bottom of the mountain.

But those symptoms were nothing compared to what I experienced now. When my eyes collided with the blue sedan at the bottom, I wanted to turn around and run. The front of the car was wrapped around a tree. How could anyone survive an accident like this?

The gas station attendant's ramblings from earlier replayed in my head like a bad movie. Something about a tragic accident on this same road five years ago. The family had all died.

Taking a deep breath, I felt renewed determination run through my veins as it hitched a ride on an abundance of adrenaline. I had to do this.

"Hello, can anyone hear me?" I called as I slid the last few feet to the bottom of the ravine. My wrist scraped over some exposed branches on the way down, but the pain didn't register. I called again, louder.

No answer.

I didn't want to do this! I didn't want to see the scene inside the mangled car. I drew in a shaky, hiccuping breath.

Reaching the driver's side door, I shined the flashlight inside. The beam flickered in my shaking hand. I counted three passengers, motionless and unresponsive to the bright light. My stomach flipped as the beam caught blood marring each pale face.

I bent over, hyperventilating and gasping for breath. I couldn't do this! They were probably already dead! I closed my eyes. "Please, God, I can't do this! Help me!"

I released my breath slowly, then quickly swung my flashlight back inside before I lost my nerve.

If you enjoyed this preview, YESTERDAY, and other books by Amanda Tru may be purchased from the same store where you purchased this book.

Happy reading!

Made in the USA
Columbia, SC
22 June 2017